The
BEACH
DOGS

ANDY JENNINGS

Hodder
Children's
Books

a division of Hodder Headline Limited

Author's note: Most of the dogs you are about to read about are real dogs that I have met at one time or another in different parts of the world. I met Catcher and her pups in Cape Hatteras, North Carolina; Donner in Puerta Vallarta, Mexico; Cabbie in Bodrum, Turkey; the blind guard dog on a plantation in Malaysia and, finally, the loveable rogue, Scratch, on Chaweng Beach, Koh Samui, Thailand. They are the real beach dogs. It was on Chaweng Beach that I first had the opportunity and time to observe the tragedies and successes of a community of stray dogs in their daily struggle for survival. I have simply placed these real life characters amongst them and allowed them to interact. I hope you enjoy reading about them as much as I have enjoyed knowing them.

Text copyright © 2000 Andy Jennings
Illustrations copyright © 2000 Paul Fisher Johnson

First published in Great Britain in 2000
by Hodder Children's Books

The right of Andy Jennings to be identified as the Author of this Work has been asserted by him in accordance with the Copyright, Designs and Patents Act 1988.

10 9 8 7 6 5 4 3 2

A Catalogue record for this book is available from the British Library

ISBN 0 340 77869 5

Typeset by Avon Dataset Ltd, Bidford-on-Avon, Warks

Printed and bound in Great Britain by
The Guernsey Press Co. Ltd, Channel Isles

Hodder Children's Books
a division of Hodder Headline Ltd
338 Euston Road
London NW1 3BH

This book is dedicated to the real Scratch, the inspiration for this story.

Contents

1

A dog's life

Catcher peered out from the vegetation, the final rivulets of water draining from her rain-sodden face, and watched intently through the mist as the approaching figure weaved its way across the beach toward her. The sudden downpour had now passed overhead and the fierce, tropical sun reappeared in the afternoon sky, boiling the grains of sand on Chaweng Beach until they released a haze that hung like a distorting mirage to the far end of the bay. It was another dog, of that she was sure, but who? Friend, or foe? His methodical sweep left her in no doubt that he was coming in search of the scraps of food he hoped the tourists – the two-legs – had left behind in their panic to escape the cloudburst.

Now she could see him clearly, but didn't recognise him

as one of the regulars. The way he moved, his lean body and gaunt face were all clear signs that he was a hungry dog. A hungry dog was an angry dog, and having already stolen the only plate of food left on the beach herself, there was the element of danger to consider for her five pups sitting in the sand hollow behind her, scraping their needle sharp teeth along the single chicken bone she had brought them. With no mate there to help protect them, a fight was the last thing she wanted.

The stranger stopped, no more than twenty yards from her, raised his head into the damp air and attempted to track the faintest of smells, as he looked in her direction.

From behind the bushes, Catcher remained perfectly still, hoping that her pups were too engaged with the bone to start their noisy squabbling again. The stranger's stare aligned with her own so that she convinced herself that she had been seen. Her muscles tensed as she readied herself for the inevitable confrontation, while her eyes studied every detail of his body language, searching for early signs of his intent. Then, quite unexpectedly, the dog turned away and continued his meandering search of the beach.

She waited until he had passed out of sight before relaxing once again, then slid herself into the sand alongside her pups. The disturbed darker sand at the centre of the hollow and the lighter sand that surrounded it matched the colouring of her own body, so that she blended perfectly into her surroundings. As she settled, the pups abandoned their now clean bone and nestled beneath her, looking for milk.

This was Catcher's third litter. Five puppies meant five hungry mouths to pull at her drying teats and yet more worries about how she was going to find enough food to survive on. Of the nine pups from her previous two litters, only three survived today. The others had died of infections, in road accidents or been shot by the dog patrol. All three now fended for themselves, but still paid the occasional visit back to their mother to renew the bond between them.

She was known as Catcher because of her skill as a rat-catcher, but she responded to most any name the two-legs chose to use, so long as there was a food reward to go with it. As a pup she'd soon learned the tone of voice that meant a dog was being called. It might not be her that was being called, but she had to be sure not to miss the opportunity to be that dog.

Rat-catching was a skill in great demand by the locals who recognised Catcher's skills in keeping the rodent population out of sight of the tourists. She patrolled the neglected back areas of the hotels and restaurants by night, stealthily tracking her prey as they rummaged through the contents of the garbage cans and bags. She enjoyed the kill, for it was her instinct to be a predator and not the scavenger that circumstance forced her to be. She was always careful to bite as close in as she could, so that the rat was unable to turn its head sideways and bite her back. Once, after a heavy rainfall, as the flooding drains and sewers had spewed out rats by the dozen, she had gone on a killing frenzy, but, getting careless, had been badly bitten on the lip, giving her a wound that had swollen and oozed for weeks afterwards.

Of course, she could have eaten the rats herself, and there had been times when she had done just that. But the best strategy was to trade them for something more edible, by waiting at a back door until one of the workers came to throw out the rubbish or take a smoke break. Having presented herself, the rat was dropped unceremoniously at their feet, while she looked expectantly up. The first time it was always the same reaction: they took a startled step back, then, seeing the dead rat, called inside to the others. Soon there were several of them standing around her until, finally, one offered some tasty morsel in exchange for her trophy. Often it was little more than leftover rice, which she ate with reluctance. But every once in a while she was given a bucket of leftovers which she could pick over or gorge upon, depending on her hunger.

Now her long, sandy eyelashes flickered gently as she tolerated the discomfort of the pups' eager feeding. *Ouch!* She pulled away and cuffed the pup who pulled too hungrily at her. At six weeks of age they were beginning to get a little too old to still want milk, but with so little else to eat, how could she blame them? With a mother's concern for her babies, she nuzzled him back into the warmth of her belly. After all, it wasn't their fault that they were so hungry. She just hadn't been able to go scavenging while caring for them, and her mate, Bouncer, was already late coming back to their makeshift den, hidden beneath a pile of discarded wooden palettes nearby.

She began to wonder if something untoward might have

happened to him. He was usually a good provider and had every indication of being the best father of any of her litters. She decided that if he wasn't back by sunset, she would have to leave the pups and go out in search of food herself.

To distract herself from the discomfort of their feeding, she closed her eyes and remembered the day when Bouncer and she had met by the crab pool:

She had just finished bringing up her second litter, happy that at last the two survivors could fend for themselves. She liked the crab pool, not as a source of food, but as a place of entertainment. It constantly amazed her how quickly the crabs scurried away when she approached. No sooner had she entered their horizon than they were scampering sideways for the nearest crevice to hide in, or instantly burying themselves in a cloud of swirling sand and water.

Like all her hunting skills, she had learned the hard way. Curious as to whether they were edible, she had suffered the ignominy of a crab claw clasped vice like on to her nose as she flicked her head from side to side in a panicked attempt to escape. She hadn't noticed the newcomer to the pool, but he had noticed her, and sat back on a rocky ledge above, watching her play. He liked the long, lighter coloured strands of hair that stood horizontally from the back of her hind legs and the playful innocence with which she pawed at the water's surface. As soon as he'd heard her shriek of pain he'd leapt from the ledge and bounded to her rescue, crunching the crab's spiny shell between his teeth. She had drawn her paws over her tender snout, then looked up at the stranger. His body language hadn't been threatening, so she'd allowed him to lick the drips of blood from her nose, then run alongside him down the beach, timing her leaps into the air to match the way he bounced excitedly about his newly-found friend. From that moment on, they had become a pair.

Catcher raised her head and looked out across the beach to see if any of the two-legs were returning now that the rain had passed over, but there were none. She had spent many, many hours observing the behaviour of the two-legs. After all, there was little else to do on those long, hot, lazy days, once the search for food had been completed. It wasn't something she did out of idle curiosity, it was part of her education, for she was a survivor who lived from day to day on her wits and cunning. Observing the two-legs had taught her the distinction between the hand that feeds and the hand that beats. As a young pup, all two-legs appeared to be the same, but as time passed she soon learnt that there were two distinct types: the ones who visited and the ones who stayed. The visitors were easy to recognise because they were almost always white-skinned, even though they turned pink or brown before they left. They had different smells too; mostly from the liquids they smeared about their bodies. Some smelt like the flowers in the forest, and others like the coconuts that littered the beach. It had always puzzled her. For how could they tell who was ready to mate if their natural smells were disg̶u̶... traits had puzzled her as well: like when they drew back their lips to show their teeth in times of happiness, when to a dog this was clearly a sign of aggression. As a pup she had learnt to stand on her hind legs and reach up to her mother's mouth in the hope of receiving food, but when she had tried the same tactic with the two-legs, they had reacted as though she was attacking them, and retreated in alarm. Later, she learnt from watching the older dogs that to succeed with this tactic, you had to raise yourself at a short distance from the two-leg and hold the pose for as long as possible. Only then was a thrown offering of food possible.

The two-legs that stayed had fewer smells – mostly of food or sweat – and they were the ones that a dog had to be wary of. Practically every kick on her ribs, or stone that struck her bone-stretched hide, had come from one of them. She had learnt that lesson quickly and treated all with caution until she knew better.

Every once in a while, she met a kind two-leg who befriended her, and for a while made her a part of their family. But they always went away, leaving her back where she had started. Sometimes she had thought it would be different. This time they would take her with them. But they never did. While she was with them, her body grew a little firmer and she learnt to relax, knowing that she didn't have to worry about food for a while. Then, suddenly, they were gone, never to be seen again. What little fat she had gained soon wore off and all too soon her bones were pushing back out from beneath her skin, p in knots as it shrank back down ...raps she lived upon once more, and ...again back on the beach, competing with ... She'd remember them for a while, hoping ...she'd see them again, but it never happened. She'd remember their smell and, sometimes, would rush up to strangers to check their scent, thinking she had found them. But she never succeeded in finding them again. Still, she had to try, she had to keep believing that one day it would happen for her, otherwise she might just as well give up now and sit in the busy road. It was desperation. There had to be a way out of this life if only she could find it.

Life on the beach was tough, really tough, and Catcher had learnt the tactics of survival from many years of living from one day to the next. When there was food, she ate it, gorging herself or trying to hide it somewhere where it wouldn't be sniffed out by another dog before her return.

Natural enemies were few. Most died under the wheels of lorries or were poisoned by the rotten food they ate or which the two-legs deliberately laid out as bait for them, crawling off to die slowly and painfully amongst the undergrowth. She had heard such dogs cry their distress to deaf ears for two or more days before finally letting go. It was a hardening process that she and all the young dogs had gone through: to hear the plea for help and know not to respond to it, even though one day it could be herself in the same position. Sometimes an individual became unable to fend for itself following an injury and slowly starved to death. They came begging from the other dogs but, with so little to go around, it was a foolish dog which risked its own survival for someone who was going to die anyway. A dog that wanted to survive had to learn to ignore the pleading in their eyes and look right through the weak in their midst, as though they were invisible, and get on with satisfying the rumbling in their own stomach. And, as the population had grown over the years, that sole, day-long task had become even harder. Catcher had her problems, but like most of the older dogs, she wouldn't swap places with the young pups, for they would inherit a harder life than she had ever known.

Here, alongside her den, she was relatively safe. Having marked out the boundary of her territory with her own distinctive scent, she knew that no dog would intrude without being aware that a fight was inevitable. The same principle applied to when she ventured into their territory, resulting in a patchwork of no go areas around which all dogs had to navigate or cross at their peril. This was particularly so in relation to the areas of beach that belonged to the 'patrol dogs'. Universally despised by all beach dogs, they were traitors to their own kind who worked for the local two-legs in return for a full stomach and somewhere to call home. Their diet gave them the bulk and stamina to out-run and out-fight any beach dog fool enough to stray into their territory. They had no loyalty other than to their masters and bit into an intruder's flesh at the slightest opportunity. But most important of all, they wore the shiny disc around their necks that protected them from the 'thunder-sticks'.

Every second or third rainy season, when the number of beach dogs had grown to an embarrassing presence, the local authority sent in the marksmen. As they roamed along the beach – first thing in the morning and late in the evening – the beach dogs hid, shivering with fear as they watched for the sticks that roared like thunder and shot rods of lightning into a dog's body that made them shudder and scream. The marksmen stalked their prey like hunters around the back streets and alleyways, with the roar of their guns driving a panicked stampede of dogs into the path of another marksman concealed further along. Later, after the silence had returned, so too did the marksmen, with their flat-back truck to load the bleeding carcasses into. But the conspicuously well-fed patrol dogs, who had been given the protection of the silver disc by their two-leg masters, were spared. They could pass by the truck with impunity, and they knew it. Catcher had seen them following in the wake of the truck as it was loaded, sniffing the puddles of blood and looking curiously on to see who they would no longer have to chase from their patch of beach.

As a pup, she had been terrified to see her mother running full speed away from the den, trying to draw the hunters away from her young. The thunder-stick had roared, her shoulder had burst open and she'd collapsed on to the ground, her rear legs driving on so that she had slid and spun in her own blood. Catcher had never been able to erase that image from her memory, nor how she had shivered amongst her brothers and sisters as they watched her twitching body being dragged away by the tail, leaving a trail of warm, thick blood seeping into the ground that they later followed until it ended abruptly beside the road. Even now, whenever a thunderstorm passes overhead, she remembers that day and once again feels the uncontrollable shivers pass through her body. She hates storms.

It was a lonely life too, for they were all rivals, with little room for companionship when everyone was joined in the same daily struggle for survival. But in one respect, however, they were allies. When the thunder-sticks were seen, even before the lightning struck, dog called to dog all along the beach, to warn of the danger, each hoping that they wouldn't be one of the heap of twisted bodies to be taken from the beach that day. Catcher had often thought it strange that no matter how hard the life they endured was, when the opportunity for a quick exit from their suffering presented itself, she and the others ran away to hide from it. But for how much longer could she go on? Every day there seemed to be more mouths to feed and less food. Then the thunder-sticks came along and, for those who escaped, life was a little easier for a while.

She nuzzled the now sleeping litter closer to one another and pulled herself carefully out of the hollow. But she didn't leave. Instead, she sat alongside, waiting to ensure that no adventurous pup followed after her.

As the long shadows of the trees began to stretch with

the setting sun, she prepared herself to go in search of Bouncer. In the distance a twig snapped and she tensed herself as she smelt the air for scent. Then, recognising Bouncer's smell she ran forward in greeting, licking him anxiously around his mouth and the small bone that it contained. He acknowledged her and circled several times around her, before continuing to the pups where his first duty lay. As he fell exhausted amongst them, the young pups gathered feverishly around to suck and chew the thin shreds of meat that hung from the bone he presented them.

While the others fought over the bone, one pup sat back, alone and disinterested, too tired even to claim her share. Catcher had given no name to this runt of the litter, for without doubt she would soon be dead. The others were named by their most obvious trait: Snarl for his attitude, Sandy for his colour, Tag for his follow-the-leader character, and Lady for her manners. The runt was the smallest and always the last to feed after the stronger siblings had forced her to one side. That was nature's way – survival of the fittest – and Catcher knew that to be as true in the den as in the cruel world outside. She knew that she shouldn't intervene, but every once in a while, couldn't help but pity the youngest and her valiant efforts to survive. On several occasions she had pulled her away from the squabble for food that she would inevitably lose, and kept a piece of meat back just for her. Bouncer had seen her doing it once, and nipped the back of her leg to remind her of her duty to the others. After all, if she couldn't out-manoeuvre her brothers and sister, what chance did she have in the outside world of two-legs and patrol dogs?

Catcher had noticed the infection growing in the youngest's eye for several days now. Possibly a speck of dry grass had blown in, causing irritation of the delicate tissue. She knew the pup needed help but didn't want to be seen to be giving her special attention for fear of causing jealousy amongst the others. And so she waited until the bone had been stripped clean before taking the pups, one at a time, and conspicuously cleaning each one, paying special attention to the head and face. She began with Snarl, the eldest, then worked her way down the line until she could clear the pus from the youngest's eye without drawing attention to her. Snarl was clearly aware of his position of dominance in the litter and was always practising his aggressive snarl on the others whenever he wanted to get his own way. Instinctively he knew that this single tactic would be the most decisive element in the many future confrontations he would have.

When the youngest's turn came, Catcher carefully worked her way around the edges of the eye, securing the irritated pup in position with a paw across the back of her neck. But if something was lodged in there, her broad, soft tongue wasn't the right tool to remove it. As she probed, the pup yelped intermittently as the movement drove the tiny barbs deeper into her eye. There was nothing more her mother could do than offer token comfort and cosmetic improvement. In time, the pup would go blind.

Bouncer watched the pair with a sidelong glance.

He had to be tough and detached – after all he was supposed to set an example for the youngsters to learn from. Nevertheless, he too felt a sadness that his youngest was in slow decline and prepared himself for the inevitable. The four other pups began to notice the greater attentiveness with which their mother groomed the youngest and, agitated, they began to rally around her, demanding their share as well. Seeing the problem, Bouncer pushed his nose though them like a plough, sending them tumbling on either side of him. There was nothing they enjoyed more than a rough and tumble with their father, with the result that they soon lost interest in their younger sister as they entangled themselves in a writhing heap of legs and tails. It was a game, but a game with a purpose, for they continually learnt new tactics as they stretched and strengthened their young muscles.

Once the meal and clean-up were over, Catcher led them into the den and settled them down for the night. By the time they eventually fell asleep in a jumble of bodies, the sun had already passed below the horizon and darkness had closed in.

Catcher joined Bouncer back in the sand hollow and took hold of the other end of the bare bone that he was chewing. It wasn't much to show for a whole day spent scavenging, but Catcher knew that she should be grateful, for some days he came back with nothing at all, and then the family had to try and sleep with rumbling, empty stomachs, while she went in search of rats. They spent the remainder of the evening reducing the bone to manageable splinters, until Bouncer, having spent a tiring day constantly on the move, fell asleep alongside her. Without disturbing his rest, she carefully rose to her feet and set off towards the hotels in search of rats.

Scavenging by night was probably the safest option, for she knew that the patrol dogs would have gorged themselves on the bowls full of leftovers from their masters' kitchens and be sleeping off their full stomachs in some quite corner. But against that had to be set the fact that other beach dogs had spent the entire day rooting out what scraps the passing day had produced. All that remained now was the remnants of the day's final meal. Years ago it had been the practice of the hotels and restaurants to leave their waste outside in plastic bags and boxes while awaiting collection, but with the increase in tourism their procedures had changed. Now, they placed their refuse in large, heavy-lidded, metal containers that were periodically emptied into the back of visiting trucks. Catcher knew from fruitless attempts that she hadn't the strength to prise open the lids of these containers, but every once in a while one would be filled to overflowing, allowing her to squeeze beneath the lid and rummage through the contents. Within those containers was food enough to satisfy the stomachs of most of Chaweng's beach dogs, yet the two-legs preferred to throw it away rather than let them feed upon it.

Passing through the back yards of several neighbouring hotels, she found only closed containers and was beginning to despair when she saw a pair of rats run across the car park towards a low wall that surrounded a gas tank. She followed, using the cover of parked cars to conceal her approach, and settled close by. From behind the wall she heard the distinctive rustle of plastic bags and smelt the greasy aroma of kitchen scraps.

Immediately she approached, a half dozen rats scurried for cover beneath the tank, leaving her to inspect the contents of the bin bag that had been dumped there. She would now have to make a judgement as to which would be the more rewarding. Sometimes, when the pickings were good, she would rummage alongside them, the rats somehow sensing that she was as hungry as they, and therefore not a threat to them. At other times, her disinterest in them was a cunning ploy; a trap she lured them into. This was one of those occasions. The bag contained only a few chicken carcasses, notorious for the thin, splintery bones that could lodge in her throat. She feigned interest in the contents, pushing her nose anxiously through it and exaggerating the chewing movements of her jaw. One by one, the rats returned and cautiously scavenged alongside her. Satisfied that they were too preoccupied to notice, she scanned them for the fattest member, waited until the sound of their gnawing through cardboard and plastic wrappings drowned her approach, then struck. Biting hard behind the neck with her front teeth, she shook the rat violently from side to side in a figure of eight movement, until the struggling rodent went limp. The others immediately scattered in all directions, squealing like miniature pigs in their blind panic to escape the same fate.

Holding the dead rat between her teeth, she set off toward the back door of the hotel kitchen. Sooner or later, one of the white clothed workers would come to the door to throw out some rubbish or take a smoke break. She sat patiently nearby, the lifeless, black body lying passively alongside, and waited.

After half an hour, a dim light flicked on above the door and the handle began to turn. Catcher picked up the rat and sat upright in anticipation, readying herself for the creak of rusty hinges and the arc of white light which swept across the shadows.

This particular hotel kitchen was one of her regular 'trading posts' and the routine was well established. Where she caught the rat was not where she would necessarily deliver it. Some back doors were more generous than others, and so, by her deliveries, it was those back doors which came to believe they had a major rodent problem.

The kitchen porter looked down and acknowledged her presence with a nod of his head, then sat down on the doorstep with his bag of rubbish and lit a cigarette. In the flickering yellow flame of his match, she watched his face, waiting for the signal. As she waited for him to finish his cigarette, doubts began to pass through her mind whether he was going to accept her offering. Such was her hunger that even these few short moments seemed to put an edge on the craving within her.

Finally, he stubbed the cigarette out on the step and made the gesture: an upward jutting of his chin toward her, as if pointing with it at the rat she patiently held in her mouth. Catcher came forward and dropped it at his feet. He lowered the sole of his shoe across its middle and pressed down, as if judging its bulk. Suitably impressed,

17

he nodded to acknowledge its worth and, bringing the open rubbish bag alongside, casually kicked it in. While Catcher anxiously waited, he lifted the lid to the rubbish container, threw the bag inside and returned to the kitchen with not a word said.

Yet more precious moments passed as Catcher listened intently for sounds of his return. Ten minutes passed and she began to give up hope but, reassured by the fact that the light had been left on, she remained.

Another ten minutes and nothing.

Finally, she gave up hope of receiving her reward, wondering if she would have been wiser to have taken the rat home to eat. She was some thirty yards away when the sound of the creaking hinge made her turn. A plastic bucket was lowered unceremoniously on to the back step and the door slammed shut once more. She sprang forward, at once concerned that some other dog might be nearby to steal her prize.

Within the bucket there lay a jumbled assortment of the day's menu, from cumbersome melon rinds to gritty, after-dinner coffee grounds. Some items – like desserts – she nosed to one side, in search of the meat that she could smell beneath. Others – like raw offal – she lifted out and dropped into a small pile on the concrete, instinctively knowing that it would nourish her young family. Before returning to the bucket each time, she glanced to her rear, ever mindful of the presence of other, equally hungry dogs. Having judged and apportioned the contents, she set about satisfying her hunger and bolted down the remnants. This was no time to savour her food as she had done earlier with the bone, for other prowling dogs would soon pick up the scent of her success and want to challenge her. Leaving the fruit skins and other rejects to one side, she licked the bucket clean, then set about loading her mouth with her prime selection. She filled it to capacity, but still a few scraps remained. Rather than leave it, she set the whole lot down, ate the scraps, then recharged her mouth and left.

It wasn't easy to breathe with a mouthful of food and, by the time she arrived back at the den, she was panting so noisily through her nostrils that it woke the pups. They stood high on their rear legs, reaching up to the mouth that they knew contained food and licking her lips feverishly. She dropped the contents before them then, recovering half, took it outside and lay it before Bouncer.

At first he was reluctant to accept it, but seeing the swell of her stomach and hearing the feeding frenzy in the den, he knew that the priorities had been taken care of and lifted the offering into his mouth.

Such is a day in the life of a beach dog.

2

Scratch

Scratch knew that his days were numbered. He was becoming ever more tired, no matter how much he slept, and the stamina he needed to struggle from one day to the next was slowly dwindling. He'd considered walking out in front of the thunder-sticks; offering himself to them and escaping from the tormented life he led. Yet somehow, no matter how hard his life was, he carried on. He'd thought about that quite a lot lately. With such long, empty days there was ample opportunity for him to indulge in his thoughts and to wonder why he allowed himself to suffer so much. This large, ungainly, old dog had somehow managed to survive to the age when his joints constantly ached and he ran out of breath with only the slightest of effort. In his time he'd seen dogs come and go. Most died young, but a few, like him, made it through to the stage in life when they began to feel like giving up. Carrying on had become such an effort that it hardly seemed worth it anymore.

Like all beach dogs he was a mongrel; the result of generations of cross breeding. Yet somewhere in that confused lineage, there was an echo from the past, for it was plain to see that his awkward size, flopping ears and drooping eyes bore some resemblance to a bloodhound. Some dogs were so distinctive that their names spoke for themselves, and Scratch certainly lived up to his. He seemed incapable of spending more than thirty seconds without scratching some part of his anatomy. As a pup he'd caught an infection that was so irritating that his constant scratching progressively caused almost all of his hair to fall out, except for the few tufts that persisted around the rim of his ears and a mohican-like ridge that ran along the top of his back where he found it most difficult to reach. His exposed skin hadn't weathered well under the fierce sun, the onslaught of insects and the fungal infections that he'd picked up from scavenging in piles of refuse. Now his blotchy, pink skin was a patchwork of fresh wounds and old scars that remained a constant source of irritation, and drove him crazy at times. Sometimes he stayed awake all night, constantly scratching and nibbling at his flesh until it tore, yet such was the satisfaction he got from it that at times he whined with intermingled tones of pain and pleasure. As if such disfigurement wasn't enough to contend with, he had also been born with a protruding lower jaw that caused his lower front teeth to jut up in front of his upper lip, giving him a comic appearance. A dog like Scratch wasn't one that could easily be forgotten.

Scratch kept to himself, well that's how he liked to think of it. The truth was that he was so old, that he'd be a liability to anyone foolish enough to befriend him. But there was another reason too. His sickly appearance had always made him repulsive to dogs and two-legs alike, and an easy target for the patrol dogs who guarded certain stretches of the beach where the best pickings were to be had from the visiting two-legs.

Today, as he made his way along the shady side of a dusty, back alley toward the beach, he glanced casually at the other dogs who gave him a wide berth, their manner clearly demonstrating their fear that his illness might also blight them. This was going to be a day much like any other. The monotony of the climate meant that every day followed the same pattern, day in, day out. It was only when the rains came that there was any variety and some welcome relief for his troublesome skin. The cooling caress of rain would soothe the irritation away, allowing him to sleep in peace for once. But there was a penalty to pay, for during the long rains the visiting two-legs would stay away, and so there was less food to go around. That meant more competition for what little food remained, which in turn meant more injuries. It wasn't simply a matter of *being* the best fighter, it was a matter of making others *think* that you were. If you could put on a good enough show of bared teeth and raised hackles, if you could reverberate your growls through a deep chest and posture aggressively, then the prize would be yours without a fight. In his younger days, Scratch had been good at such deception, and for a number of years it had worked. But once his bluff had been called and he had been severely mauled by a newcomer to the beach, word had soon spread that he was not so tough after all and others were no longer prepared to give in to his intimidation. From then on he had to consider how much injury he was prepared to sustain in order to win a scrap of food. Maybe he could win, but an injury might weaken him for further challenges. A visible wound would immediately lower his status in the pecking order of beach dogs and the younger males, ever looking to improve their ranking, would be more inclined to challenge him. Even assuming he made a full recovery, he would then have to reassert himself all over again in order to regain his former status.

A few years ago, that had been precisely the situation he had found himself in when his skin disease had deteriorated and the loss of hair meant that he no longer had a barrier to cushion the jab and tear of an attacker's teeth. Now when he raised his formerly fearsome hackles, nothing more than pink wrinkles emerged. Unable to win back his status, he needed an alternative strategy if he was to avoid slow starvation and death. And so he devised the 'pity' factor.

Leaving the alley that led out on to the beach, he approached one of the smaller hotels where there were no patrol dogs to harass him. It was a popular spot with beach dogs for that simple reason, but it had to be balanced against the effect of competition. Fights and squabbles amongst the beach dogs were frequent and injuries were something he could ill afford to take at his ripe, old age. Scattered here and there were several wooden sunloungers, parasols and the inevitable small tables laden with drinks and snacks for the two-legs basking beneath the sun. Dotted around the perimeter sat three or four beach dogs, waiting impatiently for a thrown offering, or anticipating the moment when they could wander casually past the tables and pull the leftovers from the paper plates. Torn between the hunger in their stomachs and the memory of past beatings from irate two-legs, they sat indecisively, watching each other as much as the tables.

The other dogs watched in unison as Scratch crossed the beach towards the two-legs and, ignoring the tables, settled in the sand amongst them. Making no effort to even acknowledge the presence of food nearby, he lowered himself down with a practised, world-weary sigh that was almost human, for Scratch had developed his acting skills as well as any two-leg on the hotel cabaret nights. His unique appearance rarely went unnoticed and inevitably fingers would point and comment would be passed about the strange-looking dog nearby. Turning on the spot, as if to make himself comfortable, he presented his deformities full circle, like a practised beggar, raised his head to show his protruding teeth and observed the now familiar mixed expressions of amusement and repulsion upon the faces of his audience. Twenty yards or so away, the other dogs looked on, anxious to rush forward the moment any food was offered to him.

With distinctive folds of speckled pink skin hanging beneath his droopy eyes, Scratch lowered his head and looked despondently about him, as if peering over the frames of non existent glasses, and lowered himself on to the sand once more with forelegs trembling under the strain of the effort. He closed his eyes as if oblivious of his whereabouts and sighed aloud one final time. Keeping his breathing as shallow as possible, he remained perfectly still.

As minutes passed, concern spread amongst the two-legs about the dog that had died before them. Voices called to him, quietly at first, then a whistle or two, but Scratch remained motionless throughout.

Hearing the calls, the other dogs raised themselves to their feet, hoping the call was for them, but no one looked in their direction, only at the still, pink form curled into the sand.

Inevitably, a two-leg approached and not wanting to touch the infested carcass with his hand, prodded it with his foot. Scratch rolled with a dead weight motion that dropped the side of his head on to the sand with the tip of his tongue hanging motionless from his mouth. He could hear the voices increase in pitch and number until finally a cup of water was emptied on to his face. He controlled his urge to react to the shock of contact and waited precious moments before half raising an eyelid. A sigh of relief passed amongst his audience and someone dared to stroke a hand reassuringly upon his head. So far so good. He had now won their sympathy. Moments later, his sensitive nose detected the aroma of hot food nearby, but he refused to allow his nostrils to twitch in response. As the food was offered to his mouth, his lazy tongue half-heartedly played with it, while inside his instinct was to snatch it and run. Raising his head from the sand, he opened both eyes, pinned his ears back and began to shiver his body as if expecting a beating.

As the other dogs curiously approached the gathering, they were chased back by several arm-waving two-legs, while at its centre, a now partially recovered Scratch was accepting a variety of offerings from his saviours.

It was normally the female two-legs who were most sympathetic to his plight. And such displays would invariably encourage them to bring small bags of food scraps to the beach for him. Each was treated as someone special; as though she was the only one ever to help him. He would remember them, by sight and smell, so that whenever they approached he could make a conspicuous effort to raise his weary, old body and hobble towards them in greeting. It made them feel good to be recognised and gave them a reward for their charity. But he knew it was only temporary and in a week or two's time when they had gone, he would have to erase them from his memory and start afresh on the new arrivals.

Next morning, Scratch took it easy and lazed in the shade alongside one of the beach huts long after he would have normally set out scavenging. After all, his stomach was still comfortably full from yesterday's success.

It was a pleasant day, with a gentle sea breeze that was picking up in strength. Out to sea, white crests were forming along the distant waves well before they broke on to the beach. Yesterday's rain had been the first for some time and a sign of the changing season to come. Scratch knew from years of experience the constantly repeating cycle of monsoon weather. From now on both wind and rain would increase until they combined to wreak havoc for days on end. That would be a difficult time for all the dogs of Chaweng Beach, including crafty, old Scratch, for the two-legs would stay away and the scraps would disappear.

Not until mid-afternoon did he start to feel hungry again, and set off for the hotel complex at the far end of the beach. It consisted of several large hotels that led straight on to the beach, each with their own resident patrol dogs to guard their particular stretch. To the two-legs who dotted the sands it was a continuous area of beach, but to the beach dogs it was a patchwork of territories, divided up by a series of invisible lines and punctuated by the various patrol dogs' urine markings around the perimeter of their particular section. Any beach dog that ventured into that territory was asking for trouble, for once you had crossed into the first, you stood the chance of being chased from one plot to the next and from one patrol dog to the next. The only neutral territory that then remained was the sea.

Scratch was feeling lucky after yesterday's success and considered which of his many strategies he would use today. He'd found from experience that some of the male two-legs were dismissive of him and came to realise that they had no respect for a dog that whimpered and lay on its stomach like a snake. They were males like him and responded to male instincts, and so he had to set about stimulating their instinct for fair play.

Eventually he reached the perimeter of the hotel area and observed a small group of beach dogs wandering to and fro in nervous anticipation of going further. He joined them, but instead of pacing nervously alongside them, he sat and waited until a couple of the local food vendors passed by. Sheltering their heads from the heat of the sun beneath their wide-brimmed straw hats, they carried a pole across their shoulders slung with burning coals in a brazier at one end and a mobile kitchen at the other. Setting on the sand beside their customer, they would fan the coals bright red and grill sticks laden with cubes of meat, fish or chicken wings. The smell that carried on the breeze was torture to a hungry dog and was sure to attract competition. Scratch's strategy was simple: he would follow them from the safety of the shoreline on to the first plot, wait until the patrol dogs emerged, attracted by the smell of food and, knowing it was their duty to protect their master's stretch of sand from scavengers, then use his cunning to take the prize.

As the vendors passed by, the mix and match collection of beach dogs moved down to the shoreline and kept a parallel course. Whenever the vendors stopped beside a prospective customer, so too did the dogs, settling in the damp sand and watching their every move.

Meanwhile, from within the hotel grounds, the patrol dogs emerged on cue and positioned themselves nearby, but not so close as to annoy the tourists, for they knew that their masters disliked them begging for scraps like a beach dog. Anyway, they were well-fed with leftovers from the kitchen twice a day.

The scene was now set and the beach dogs began to inch hesitantly forward from the sea toward the invisible line that once crossed meant a challenge from a patrol dog. Their hunger drove them on, each reluctant to concede the slightest of advances made by a competitor. Yet Scratch, seemingly unconcerned, remained at the rear.

The patrol dogs raised themselves from sitting, flexing their muscles like well-trained athletes for the event to come; the victors of which were in no doubt. Then, from amongst the beach dogs, Scratch emerged, leaving the water's edge and apparently oblivious to the tension around him, like the village idiot they all considered him to be. The patrol dogs disliked him, for he left a bad taste in their mouth. When they bit other dogs, they savoured the salty tang of blood, but Scratch left them coughing up the flakes of dried skin that crumbled away from his body. They preferred to leave Scratch to their master who kept his catapult and stones beneath the counter for just such occasions.

Scratch ambled carelessly up the beach whilst looking sideways through half-closed eyes, until he could see the two-leg emerge from behind the beachside bar with his weapon in hand. Experience had taught him the range at which it was accurate, so he took care to pace his approach until such time as he had conjured up a small audience for his performance. Although he obviously preferred not to be hit with the stone, it mattered not whether he was, for his reaction was the same. Having satisfied himself that his sickly appearance had generated sufficient interest from the two-legs, he diverted closer to the bar and awaited the 'thwang' of recoiling rubber that sent a stone hurtling in his direction. Timing its flight, he yelped aloud at the precise moment that contact could have been expected. It was a yelp of startled pain, an unexpected high pitched attention grabber directed at his audience and held just long enough to turn all heads. Now that he had their attention, he followed through with a succession of yelps as he feigned a limp, and made for the cover of the trees. His practised three-legged scamper, with the fourth held high and immobile drew sighs of sympathy from the onlookers and angry protestation to the barman who took great pride in what he believed to be his accuracy.

Beyond the range of the patrol dogs, he entered the trees that backed on to the beach, allowing himself to remain just in view as he licked and inspected his injury. Sometimes it would only be a matter of minutes, sometimes an hour or more, but invariably curiosity would get the better of one of the tourists and he would be visited.

Sure enough, within about ten minutes some two-legs came his way. As they approached he dragged himself away, whimpering as he pulled his limp hind leg behind him. Eventually he succumbed to their cooing tones and sniffed their offered, open hand. Playing on his hairless appearance, he ducked his head as they tried to touch him, as though ashamed of his ugliness. Patiently, he allowed them to touch his injured leg, emitting the occasional cry of distress as their fingertips prodded the bones within. Reassuring words were said as yet more of them gathered around him. Then came the smell on the wind as his reward was offered from amongst them. A paper napkin was placed beside his head, holding assorted food scraps that had been hastily gathered together for the wounded animal. Much as he wanted to gulp it down in one go, he resisted and, holding his head barely off the ground, lifted the morsels into his mouth. This was luxury indeed, for there was no gritty sand in it, like most of the scraps thrown to him.

After some moments of half-hearted eating, he summoned himself to his feet and practised walking like a newborn deer, gingerly lowering his fourth leg several times until it would finally bear his weight. Initially moving away from them, he cautiously returned, loaded the remaining food into his mouth and carried it off into the undergrowth beyond.

A foolish dog would use that ruse once too often and lose credibility, but like all good actors, Scratch limited his performances. It was just one of a repertoire of tactics he'd developed over the years. That single performance would reward him with scraps brought to his gap in the trees for days or weeks to come. It was just one more way to survive.

3

Donner

It was a particularly hot afternoon and Catcher lay panting in the makeshift den with her splay-legged pups arranged around her. Some days seemed to be exceptionally hot and, unlike the tourists who seemed to enjoy it all the more, all a dog wanted to do was find a cool, shady spot and sleep. There was little Catcher could do to relieve the discomfort of the weather. The den had been chosen for reasons of security, not comfort, and they would just have to suffer. To her surprise, it was not the youngest pup, but the second eldest, Sandy, who suffered most from the heat. His breathing had become very erratic. At times it was very fast and shallow, while at others it was so slow and quiet that she had to nudge him with her nose to check he was still alive. With several hours to go before the heat

32

of the day would begin to subside, Catcher decided to take him outside where a slight breeze stirred. She waited until Bouncer had returned from his morning's scavenging before closing her jaws around the loose flesh on the back of Sandy's neck and lifting him outside. Placing him on the scorched, barren dirt, she encouraged him to follow her to the rear of a nearby hotel compound. At first his sleep-weary legs buckled beneath him, sending him in a series of clumsy stumbles, but as he got into his stride he began to take an interest in the world outside, looking curiously about himself and sniffing every new scent that passed across his path.

A tunnel ran at dog height through the undergrowth that clung to the whitewashed perimeter wall of the hotel complex. Years of constant to-ing and fro-ing had created the body hugging, hidden highway that protected the beach dogs as they roamed. To the dogs it was a criss-cross pattern of trails and boundaries, signposted by a myriad, invisible scents. Each dog carried his own unique mind map that guided him between friend and foe, and separated the safe and dangerous areas.

As they approached close to the rear of the compound, Catcher slowed and moved cautiously forward, sniffing for any trace of the patrol dogs who guarded the rear entrance. Not prepared to move with her weak youngster until she was satisfied it was safe, she lowered herself to the ground with ears raised and waited. Of all the pups, Sandy had the fairest fur, and so shared his mother's advantage of being able to blend in with the beach and not be seen. But here, amidst the lush, green vegetation, their colouring was a liability.

Once satisfied that the patrol dogs were elsewhere, Catcher came out from cover, darted quickly through the rear gate and into one of the hedges that shielded the large fuel tanks. Close on her heels, Sandy sensed the adventure and copied her every move. Pushing beneath the lower branches of the hedge, they emerged in a spot where two lines of trees that skirted each side of the hotel joined together at the rear. They formed a natural wind tunnel that channelled the daytime sea breeze up through the hotel grounds to precisely that spot. They settled, side by side, in the shadow of a waste compactor and enjoyed the cooling flow of air about them. It took several minutes for Sandy's breathing to recover from the exertion of the journey, but he soon settled into a peaceful doze.

Catcher couldn't afford such a luxury and remained alert for early warning of anyone's approach. She had taken a calculated risk in coming here, for if one of the patrol dogs found her, escape would be hard. The rear of the complex was a high-walled dead-end which she could jump only with difficulty. Sandy certainly couldn't. Similarly, she might outrun an overweight patrol dog over a short distance, but her pup certainly couldn't. In her favour were two things: first was the fact that the hotel dogs rarely patrolled the back areas, concentrating on the more conspicuous beach area where they could impress their master, and secondly, she was upwind of them and therefore able to catch their scent while they could not trace hers.

* * *

Two hours later and the intensity of the afternoon heat had noticeably declined. She prodded Sandy's side with her nose to awaken him from his sleep and waited as he stood up and urinated against a nearby shrub, while she kept her eyes trained on the hotel. Just as she was about to lead the way back she caught the faintest scent blowing up through the hotel grounds and immediately lowered herself and watched intently. Sandy copied her. Nothing moved for several moments as the scent cleared but, ever cautious, she retreated into the shrubs and continued to peer out from within.

Blitzen the Dobermann walked aimlessly along the footpath that led to the rear of the hotel. He was bored. Nobody wanted to play with him and, thanks to the heat, there were no beach dogs about either. He looked towards the garbage compactor, suddenly remembering that he had once chased some rats from beneath it earlier in the year.

Catcher and her pup remained frozen, their eyes riveted on his muscular torso. Sandy knew instinctively from his mother's body language that they were in grave danger and, remaining pressed close to her side, began to shiver with fear.

Blitzen passed within ten yards of where they had been lying, casting his eyes down low and sweeping his head from side to side as though looking for them. He stopped at the compactor and circled it slowly several times before settling down in the shade nearby, sighing with boredom as he lowered his head on to his outstretched paws.

Catcher realised that they had not been discovered. Had

the wind been blowing in a different direction she would surely have had a fight on her hands by now. After five minutes of patient observation, she began to move sideways through the undergrowth with Sandy close behind. But the inexperienced Sandy wasn't paying attention to his footfalls. A brittle twig snapped beneath his paw and Blitzen's head immediately rose and turned in their direction, his erect ears swivelling from side to side to pinpoint the source. Catcher froze. He seemed to be looking straight at her with those piercing black eyes, but she knew better than to make a bolt for it.

Blitzen continued to stare into the shadows, hoping to see a rat, until the eye strain caused him to blink. He saw nothing and wasn't prepared to expend any more energy in the pursuit of such worthless prey. Turning away, he lowered his head on to his paws once more to return to his rest. For a brief moment the wind dropped, then backed on itself, before turning again. In that briefest of moments he caught the scent of another dog nearby. He immediately sprang to his feet, but sniff as he might, he couldn't get a direction or any other trace of the scent and began to wonder whether he'd imagined it.

Catcher felt the tension grow within her as the Dobermann began to walk slowly in their direction. Another step or two and he would surely see them. As the dog turned toward the shrub, she suddenly recalled that Sandy had urinated there. Blitzen gave a series of double snorts as his nostrils drank in the freshly caught scent and tracked its source. She had a plan: at the first sign that he had actually found them, she would grab Sandy by the neck and run for her life directly into the hotel. If she could just make it to the area where she had seen the two-legs sitting together in groups, she would be relatively safe, for she knew they were more sympathetic to a beach dog's plight than the locals who would enjoy the spectacle of a dog fight. Hopefully one of them would take pity on her, or at least her pup, and rescue them from the jaws of the Dobermann. She might have to take a bite or two and a beating from a broom, but that was preferable to the full onslaught of an angry patrol dog and the loss of a pup.

Just then a crash sounded out from the hotel as a beer bottle fell from a tray. Blitzen's head immediately swung away from the undergrowth and in the direction of the noise. It was time for him to earn his keep. Perhaps it was nothing, but he knew that his presence at the scene of any disturbance would not go unnoticed by his master. A single bark of acceptance to the challenge and he bounded away.

Her heart pounding heavily within her chest and her dry tongue sticking to the roof of her mouth, Catcher relaxed the tension she had built up within her muscles and seized the opportunity given her to make good their escape. In unison she and Sandy retraced the route they had taken beneath the hedges, out of the gate and into the tunnel alongside the wall.

Blitzen joined his father, Donner, at the poolside. Standing side by side it was plain to see that they were related. Although not a pedigree like his father, he carried the near perfect body line of a Dobermann, except that his tail hadn't been docked, nor his ears cut into the standard small triangles. His sturdy, thick set chest narrowed away to a thin waist and long, muscular, rear legs that could drive him at speed. His body hair, short, fine and close, changed from light brown around his nose, through dark chocolate-brown on his chest to black at his rear end. But like all Dobermanns, his most commanding features were his teeth. Even with his mouth closed, his long canines jutted menacingly from either side of his upper lips like a vampire. Unlike other dogs who had to open their mouths to show their teeth, he could simply pull back his nose and raise the edge of his lips to display his awesome weaponry. With little more than a grimace he could establish his dominance over anyone foolish enough to challenge him.

Father and son had reached the stage of their lives whereby Blitzen was fast becoming his father's physical superior. Donner was not a young dog and had not fathered a litter until late in his life and, deep down, he knew that his days of dominance were running short. Previously, Blitzen had respected his father's example, but increasingly he was becoming less responsive to his orders and just a little slow to follow his lead. And now that he was a powerful dog in his own right, Blitzen was feeling ready to challenge his father. In the past, disagreements between them had always been settled in Donner's favour, either by Blitzen conceding to his intimidation or being physically punished for his insubordination. Donner would always have the first bite at the food; he would decide which beach dogs to chase and which to ignore and, when the time came, he would decide which bitch his son could mate with. But the day was coming ever closer when Blitzen would no longer accept his father's authority.

As the waiter swept the glass fragments into the dustpan, normality returned and the tourists readjusted themselves in their loungers. The two dogs returned to the beach, for they knew that as the sun lowered in the sky, so the tourists would return to their rooms, leaving behind them litter and scraps of food that would be rummaged through and fought over by the scavenging beach dogs.

Donner took the east side of the beach and, jutting his jaw to the west, indicated Blitzen's position. Blitzen ignored the command for a fraction too long to go unnoticed. Donner paused, jutted his jaw one final time and looked out to the west as Blitzen reluctantly obeyed. Seeing the ripples of strength in his son's muscular legs and feeling the stiffness in his own, he felt suddenly very old. Just two days ago he had lost a tooth while chewing on a bone. He knew his prime years were now past. One day soon the challenge would come, and when it did he would either have to summon what strength remained to retain his position of dominance, or face the inevitable and hand over graciously to his deserving son. But it was hard to let go, for he enjoyed being the top dog at Chaweng. As he settled in the shade of a palm tree to look out across the beach he remembered how it had all started.

His master, Karl Eidmans, was a German agricultural scientist who specialised in tropical plant diseases. And when the opportunity for a five-year secondment to the Far East had been offered to him, he had jumped at the opportunity to gain hands-on experience. Being a single man, he had no ties to hold him back, except for Donner – and leaving him behind wasn't even a consideration. Truly this man's best friend, Donner had been the welcoming bark at the front door, the lap warmer in the winter, the cold nose that woke him on a Sunday morning and the curious faced nurse who accepted his funny walk and strange behaviour when he came home drunk.

Donner was like an only child to Karl and had been spoilt from day one. Five years without his company was unthinkable. So he had been inoculated against every conceivable risk, air freighted to Thailand and cosseted through acclimatisation in an air-conditioned kennel at the agricultural research station.

But dogs will be dogs, and instinct and hormones combined to make him yearn for company of his own kind. No amount of attentive pampering could compensate for that. Whenever a full moon hung in the tropical night sky, it was accompanied by the scent of other dogs in the sticky, night air. He called expectantly into the blackness beyond the perimeter fence and at times almost believed that he could hear a response in the far distance. But only the chirping of a million insects came back.

The night forays that some of the beach dogs took were always made when the full moon was there to help them find their way through unfamiliar territory. It was on one such night that a pack of them ventured away from their seafront homes and wandered inland in search of new sources of food. Each journey took them a little further afield, navigating ever onwards using previously established landmarks for reference. One such landmark was the perimeter fence of the agricultural station, which stretched for miles and protected the experimental crops from intruders. It was there that they had heard the call of the 'devil dog', a call unlike that of any dog they had heard before. To them it was a warning from the world beyond; a warning to turn back from the unknown, hidden dangers ahead and return to the safety of the homes they had left behind.

The six foot length of dragging chain attached to Donner's collar scraped and rattled on the concrete behind him as he paced up and down the backyard. A length of stout wire ran from one end of his chain to the wall, a compromise between letting him run loose and tying him down that allowed him freedom of movement within a limited area. For over four years he had trod this same stretch of concrete, waiting anxiously for the occasional days when his master would allow him to ride in the back of the Land Rover to some of the outstations in the hills.

Tonight he was restless as his hormones tortured him, for he wanted a mate. Calling out into the night air, he stood on his hind legs and leaned his weight against the chain as he faced towards the perimeter fence and sniffed high into the air where the scent was blowing stronger over the tall grass. He called again and was sure he heard the beach dogs call back. He strained against the chain that held him from the siren's sweet lure until his collar began to choke his call. It was torture. Turning back into the rear of the compound, he rounded upon himself, charging headlong toward their call until the taut chain jerked him back bringing him to a sudden halt. They called again, and he responded again, repeating the process over and over until his neck ached. He gave one more pull and suddenly the weakest point gave way as the metal loop in his leather collar burst open, releasing the end of the chain.

Donner ran into the night, calling out between high bounds to look over the tall grass toward the fence. Driving on through the wall of virgin vegetation, he ploughed a tunnel of crumpled stems toward his goal.

Beside the fence, the beach dogs circled agitatedly, undecided as to whether to flee or stay. With each call they could hear the devil dog closing in upon them, yet such was their curiosity, they had to stay. They glanced at one another, each hoping to take a lead from the other, but confusion reigned. Their imaginations fed upon the sound of the dog thrashing its way through the grass like a runaway train. In their minds' eye he was the size of a buffalo with teeth as long as their legs.

Then he was upon them and there was instant silence as the dogs on both side of the fence froze in disbelief at what they saw. Eyes explored each other in amazement as they took the measure of one another. Never before had they seen such a dog as Donner. His shiny body rippled with muscle upon tightly packed muscle beneath a layer of fine, black-brown hair: hair so fine that it looked as though it had been painted upon his sculptured body. As dark as the night around him, the moonlight bathing in the luminous glow of his eyes, he had an awesome presence as he stood motionless before them. No beach dog would be fool enough to make the first move, for fear of it being seen as a challenge. Instead, they sniffed cautiously, curious to learn more about this magnificent creature. Here was an animal of majesty, a clear and natural born leader of the pack. The males moved closer together, forcing the pack leader, Scar, to the front, as though seeking comfort in their combined strength; while the females' lingering stares indicated their genetic desire for him to father their litter.

From the other side, Donner weighed up the situation: he could retreat and forget the whole thing; he could join the company of these dogs; or he could do his duty to his master and see them off. Lonely for contact with his own kind, he pushed the vulnerable tip of his nose through the chain link fence and sniffed.

A bitch, Cabbie, was the first to dare to come forward and, holding her nose inches away from his, returned the gesture. The hair on the back of his neck rose with an electric charge that rippled along his spine as he caught the warmth of the air from her nostrils. The other males stirred uneasily, looking at each other to see who would be first to initiate a move against him, but none did, not even Scar. Donner turned sideways to the fence and walked slowly parallel to it, his short, stumpy tail fascinating Cabbie. The bitch followed his lead until they were some yards away from the remainder of the pack, then turned again until they were head to tail, with the fence between, and exchanged scent. With no further communication, they turned in unison, face to face, lowered their shoulders and pulled at the soil beneath the fence with their claws. From each side of the fence a small hillock of loose soil was thrown up from between their rear legs until their paws touched. They stopped, pushed heads together beneath the wire and touched noses, their eyes gazing at each other. The signs were good so far. Reassured, they dug away with renewed vigour as the remainder of the dogs began to circle upon themselves, taking turns to retreat and push others to the front in nervous anticipation of what might happen once the devil dog joined them. While Cabbie threw more and more soil out from between her hind legs, Donner scrambled low beneath the wire, driving forward with his powerful back legs until his shoulders emerged on the far side. The other males chattered excitedly as he pulled free and ran in circles around his new found friend, feigning bites and yelping excitedly as they played together.

4

A hard lesson

The heat had declined over the past three days and Sandy's breathing had at last improved. Which was just as well, as Catcher was reluctant to risk another visit to the hotel compound. The youngest's eye was beginning to glaze over with a jelly-like dome that she was reluctant to disturb.

As usual, the pups were limited to exercising within a few yards of the den and then only when one or both of the parents were there. At other times they had to stay inside, making them restless and irritable with each other. First thing in the morning and last thing before sunset, they were escorted further afield and taught the lessons of survival by their dutiful parents. Catcher demonstrated her hunting skills, taking them to the lagoon to practise stalking the slow-witted frogs, avoiding using rats at this early stage for fear of injury. Meanwhile Bouncer taught self-preservation; showing the puppies how to remain alert at all times, how to catch the scent of approaching danger and how to find and use natural cover to conceal their presence. It was important for them to learn that the dog who devoted himself exclusively to the hunt, might himself become the hunted.

Today their lesson was about one of their deadliest enemies: the traffic that thundered along the road parallel to the beach. More dogs had died under the wheels of vehicles than from any other cause. Some dogs seemed to be blind to the presence of an approaching vehicle and would step obliviously into its path as though their eyes were unable to focus upon it. Yet had the moving object been another dog or a two-leg, they would have precisely calculated its distance, speed, direction and intent within seconds. How they couldn't see an object as large as a truck Bouncer didn't know.

It was early morning and the traffic was just beginning to increase as the produce vehicles coming in from the farms and villages made their deliveries to the hotel kitchens and restaurants. Bouncer sat at one end of the line of pups, while Catcher guarded the rear, their heads turning in unison as each vehicle thundered by just yards away. The youngest, with her infected eye, was out of sequence whenever vehicles came from the east, and had to rely on her hearing, despite Catcher encouraging her to turn her head until her good eye faced the opposite direction. Still without a name, she remained the weakling of the litter and was not expected to survive much longer.

With each passing vehicle they fine-tuned their appreciation of speed and distance, until the time came for a demonstration. The line of pups followed their father to a straight stretch of road where vehicles could be seen coming from some distance off. While Catcher remained with them, Bouncer moved closer to the edge of the black tarmac and emphasised the repeated stares he made in each direction with ears pricked high to detect any distant sound. The pups looked on in eager anticipation of what was to come. When all was clear, he crossed the open road in a straight line and at a good speed. From the far side he sat patiently looking back towards them.

Snarl, as with all things, wanted to be first and impatiently trod on the spot. When all was clear, Bouncer gave a single bark and Catcher nudged him forward. Copying his father's moves, he halted beside the road and, with ears raised, stared into the distance in both directions before scampering nervously across to join his father. Moments later a bus appeared in the distance and within five seconds hurtled by in a cloud of swirling dust and blue-grey smoke that momentarily hid his brothers and sisters from sight.

One after the other, the pups changed sides of the road, copying Snarl's example, until only the youngest remained on the far side with Catcher. Although the most disadvantaged, she had the benefit of going last and seeing the others' efforts. Having checked both directions with her good eye, by turning her head almost to the rear, she sat quietly and chose her moment carefully. Quite sure now that all was clear, she set her paw on to the road and looked across to the others, excited at the prospect of finally joining them.

In the distance, a farmer drove with his eyes held on the rear view mirror, double checking that there was no unseen vehicle bearing down upon his rear. He certainly didn't notice the tiny pup in the middle of the road.

Bouncer barked a warning, which Catcher echoed from the far side, but the confused pup didn't know which of the two to respond to and hesitated, standing still and looking back and forth. Then she heard the engine's roar on her blindside and felt the road shake beneath her tiny paws. The noise came out of nowhere and drowned the calls of her parents to run. The other pups joined in, calling out and stamping their feet on the spot as if trying to run for her.

Catcher knew that the time had come. It was sooner than she'd expected, but she'd already prepared herself for the inevitable loss of her youngest. There was no point in jeopardising the upbringing of the rest of the litter by making any attempt to save her. It was a cruel fact of survival that some had to die for others to live. Bouncer instinctively knew it too. In the seconds that it took to happen, he felt his body freeze into inaction. If the pup hadn't the ability to save itself now, then it would stand no chance in the cruel world of an adult beach dog.

A belch of black, sooty smoke shot from the jagged end of the rusty exhaust pipe as the farmer, now satisfied that the road was clear, stepped on the accelerator. Then it happened. A blur of something moving on the road directly ahead caught his eye. He stamped upon the brake, cursing his luck, as the tyres bit into the road, rubber squealed and the rear end began to skid sideways. His crates of fruit flew forward, bursting upon the back of his cab as the engine stalled into silence. Looking over his shoulder through the back panel window, he cursed aloud as he saw the damage to his precious cargo. Preoccupied with salvaging what remained, he hadn't seen the horror at the front end of his truck. When he eventually made his way around to the front, all that was immediately visible from beneath was the tail. Seizing it to drag the dead animal out from under his wheels, he dumped the carcass at the roadside then, seeing an approaching lorry, began to wave his arms overhead and walk toward it.

It was another ten minutes before the lorry tow-started the farmer's truck and both vehicles disappeared around the bend. Once out of sight, the dogs came out of hiding from beneath the bushes and crossed to where the body lay. Catcher looked down at the broken body and sniffed around the mouth, searching for signs of life. But there was no warm breath from the nostrils, only a trickle of blood. Bouncer's heart had been bigger than his instinct; he couldn't just sit there and watch his youngest die when there was still a chance for life, and that had been his mistake. He had broken the first rule of survival: that the strong will survive and the weak will perish. He had been weak in not allowing nature to follow its course and in doing so had reversed the outcome. For now the survivor was his sickly pup, who sat dazed and confused alongside him, desperately trying to lick life into her dead father's mouth. Now the well-being of the rest of the litter was in jeopardy for, without him, Catcher would have to work twice as hard and be twice as careful.

This had been the pups' first experience of a death within the family and naturally enough they had all assumed the runt would be the first to die, not their father. Yet there before them lay his lifeless torso, his crimson blood slowly soaking into the caked, dry earth beneath him.

Catcher allowed the pups to sniff and examine him, curious at the sight of his burst abdomen. They milled around each other, nervously seeking comfort in body contact. All except for one, the youngest. She had retreated to the far side of the body and sat alone staring into her father's rolled-up eyes. She looked up at Catcher and there was no mistaking the piercing, cold stare of her mother that said it should be her lying there, not him. That's what the eyes said and that's what she felt. If she could change places she would, then her brothers and sisters wouldn't look at her the way they did.

There was only one thing she could do now, she decided. She would have to grow up quickly and help her mother raise the others. She'd already managed to catch a frog when they'd visited the lagoon, so it couldn't be all that hard.

She crossed over to her mother, who instantly turned her back and called to the others instead. They knew by her tone that she meant immediately and sprang to her side. She sniffed each one as if accounting for them, with the exception of the youngest, then turned and led the way back into the trees. The youngest joined in at the rear, whereupon Catcher immediately stopped, turned and sprang upon her. Her teeth snapped shut across the pup's ear, causing her to squeal with pain and surprise, followed by a cuffing from her paw that knocked the pup over. Catcher stood over her unwanted child, curled her lips back to reveal her teeth and growled angrily. The pup lay submissively upon its back, hoping to appease her mother. Instead, she barked loud and angrily into the pup's tightly screwed-up face.

As quickly as it had started, it was over, and Catcher disappeared into the forest with the remainder of her litter, leaving the bewildered pup alone. She sat up and, drawing a paw over her bitten ear, saw the blood. She tasted it, then crossed to her father and licked at the blood around his nose as well. As if her guilt had not been enough already, the similarity of taste helped her to understand the pain he must have suffered. For if her ear hurt so much with so little blood, how much greater must his pain have been with so much. Not knowing what to do or where to go with her misery, she curled herself beneath his chest and sought the only source of comfort remaining.

As time and traffic passed, she considered returning to the den, but the pain in her ear reminded her of the kind of welcome she could expect. Once the natural warmth had drained from Bouncer's body, so the comfort it gave her dwindled, until she knew it was time to leave and make her own way in the world. How would she eat, she wondered. Where would she sleep? Perhaps the best thing for her to do was to walk into the road and join her father, wherever he had gone.

Eventually, it was the rumble in her stomach that finally made her leave him. She took one last look to remember him by, then set off for the only place she could think of to go, the only other place she knew how to find – the lagoon. At least there would be frogs there for her to eat, even though they tasted awful. But there was a problem in going there, for she only knew the route from the den, which meant she would have to return there first. If she was seen, she might be attacked again, but it was a risk she had to take.

As she made her way back, she could still detect traces of the others' scent along the way. Looking ahead with ears swivelling from side to side, she put into practice the skills her father had so recently taught her, little realising that she would need them so soon. She stopped in the bushes twenty yards away from the pile of jumbled wooden palettes that was home and watched for a few moments, hesitant to show herself until she was sure it was safe to cross the clearing to the path that led to the lagoon. Just as she finally came out from cover, she heard the sounds of a squabble coming from within and curiosity got the better of her. She approached hesitantly and sniffed cautiously. Looking into shadows from daylight, she could see nothing within and edged even closer.

Inside, the pups were too busy fighting amongst themselves to guard the entrance, and so didn't notice as she edged steadily forward and watched them playfully pulling a twig from each other's mouths. Snarl, as usual, was dominating the fight and yapping the loudest of all. Suddenly there was silence as all eyes turned on the intruder. Her sister, Lady, came forward, recognising the scent and seemingly friendly, but Snarl ran forward, pushing her to one side, and barked furiously. The others followed his lead and rallied around, forcing her to back away from the entrance until she was back in daylight.

She ran and ran, through the trees and across the stream, over the sands and into the swamp, with their angry voices still in her head, until her legs would carry her no further, and she dropped with a pounding heart amid the clumps of tall grass beside the lagoon.

From now on, this would be her home.

5

Kick boxer

Being the oldest dog on the beach had advantages and disadvantages for Scratch. He had perfected the art of parading his old age and sickly appearance in much the same way as a beggar would expose his deformities to public gaze, but his old age earned him little respect from the other beach dogs when food was in short supply and stomachs rumbled with the pangs of hunger.

It was at times like this that he would retreat from the beach and visit Lim, the only two-leg friend he had ever cultivated. They had shared the misery of their lives together and found comfort in giving support to someone whose need was as great as their own. His visits were infrequent, so as not to abuse the hospitality he received, and mostly in times of particular need.

Now was one of those times. Something he had eaten had given him food poisoning, resulting in stomach cramps, vomiting and diarrhoea for the past three days. Drained of energy, dehydrated and weak from not eating, he practically dragged himself through the dusty back streets to his old friend's ramshackle hut at the edge of town. Originally a small box hut, it had grown over the years with whatever scraps of timber and material Lim had managed to salvage from elsewhere. Littered with knotholes and splits, the twisted timbers carried rust streaked stains from the leaking corrugated sheets that covered the roof.

Halfway there, Scratch almost diverted to 'the lonely beach': the place where sick and injured dogs went to die. Bleached and desiccated by the relentless sun and sea, the bones that littered the beach served to remind any dog that visited of his ultimate destiny.

Lim had been a champion kick boxer in his youth, but that was forty five years ago as a fit, young seaman in the Thai Navy. Today, at sixty nine years of age, he was bald, round shouldered and toothless. His sunken mouth, flattened boxer's nose and stumbling gait were testimony to the punishment his sport had brought to his body. To the local children, he was someone to tease, an ugly man who they would run screaming from, mimicking horror. He ran a small, semi derelict bar at the edge of town where locals would gather to talk more than they drank. Very different to the bars that the fat-bellied tourists flocked to, Lim's bar was the social meeting point for the poor and unwaged.

Scratch understood that Lim was like him: old, lonely and only too well aware of the aches and pains that came with advancing years. Scratch had witnessed Lim's stumbling worsen, his body becoming ever thinner and the long periods of time he spent isolated from the other two-legs. He knew that Lim was the two-leg version of himself.

With no living relatives and no other livelihood possible, there would be no alternative for Lim but to end his days begging in the streets like a dog. But, for now, he felt secure inside his hut, surrounded by the familiar smells of sun-dried timber, stale beer and cooking oil. Familiarity such as this was a comfort, for the hut was the only tangible thing that existed in his life and a safe retreat from the outside world.

Sleep was something he needed less and less as he got older yet, ironically, he seemed to have more and more time on his hands with nothing to do but sleep. Reluctantly, he leaned back on to the mattress, closed his eyes and prayed for the escape of sleep once more.

Gathering the last of his remaining strength, Scratch scraped at Lim's back door with his claws, his whine almost inaudible. Lim heard the sound of a rat gnawing on wood and roused himself, happy for something to occupy him. Reaching for his shoe beneath the bed, he held it by the toecap and set off to hunt his prey. Crouching beside the back door, preparing to strike, he heard the tortured whine of an animal in pain.

This was no rat.

Lim pulled the door open and Scratch looked up into his old friend's eyes, barely able to raise himself from the ground where he lay. His whimper, flat ears and absence of tail wagging were all clear signs that something was very wrong.

Lim bent down and cradled the limp, hairless dog in his arms, carrying him inside. He'd given up worrying about catching an infection from Scratch years ago and cared even less about it now. Laying him on the bed, he spoke soft, reassuring words as his fingers felt the protruding ribs that pressed against the loose skin. Taking a small flashlight from the bedside cabinet, he prised open a drooping eyelid to look inside, then opened the mouth to see the tongue. He didn't know what he was looking for but had seen doctors do it to their patients, so there must be a point to it, he reasoned.

Having exhausted his first aid skills, he brought a small bowl of water for Scratch to drink, then a small plate of scraps he'd saved from the meal he'd cooked. Scratch ate lazily, his head remaining on the mattress as his tongue slid sideways on to the plate. For once he wasn't play-acting to an audience on the beach, he really was ill. Lim sensed the gravity of the dog's condition and took the tin of corned beef from the cupboard that he'd been saving for his birthday, and added it to the scraps. Not knowing what else to do, he fanned the stricken animal with an old sheet of newspaper and talked quietly to him, telling the story of how they had met that night at the boxing ring.

* * *

It had been three years ago, at the height of the tourist season when Scratch had wandered through town, curious to seek out the source of the shouts and cheers that came up through the back streets. Crawling under the tiered seating, he had watched in amazement as a pair of two-legs kicked and punched each other to the floor. Finally, one lay on his back and offered up his throat in surrender, just as a dog would do. The winner, accepting the submission, backed away amid much cheering from the onlookers. Scratch continued to watch in amazement as a series of contestants took turns to knock each other senseless, while a third two-leg in white clothes danced about them. Every so often the duo returned to the far corners of the ropes that surrounded them to sit down and be attended to by an older man with a bucket and a towel.

It was during one such rest period that one of the fighters ran from his corner and kicked his opponent in the head, sending him crashing to the floor. The audience rose to their feet, screaming aloud in protest until Scratch began to feel uneasy, unsure of the frenzy about him. Suddenly, silence fell on the crowd as the old man who had been attending the loser, ducked beneath the ropes, ran at the aggressor and pushed him headlong into the ropes. Scratch instantly became as anxious as the rest of the audience to see what happened next and, resting his front legs against a bar, raised himself to a standing position too. The fighter sprang off the ropes, turned to face the old man and threw a rapid series of punches that passed to either side of the old man's head, as if to show what would happen to him if he'd been a younger man. The man in white clothes ran between the two, separating them with his arms, only to receive a single head blow from the fighter that instantly dropped him to the floor like a falling stone. Undeterred, the old man advanced on the fighter, encouraged by the now cheering crowd. There followed a brief, intense battle as the old man ducked aside and beneath every blow the fighter threw at him, whilst repeatedly striking home with punches and kicks of his own. The roar of the crowd became deafening as finally the fighter was sent flying between the ropes and fell to the ground outside the ring. As groups of spectators surged forward, Scratch lost sight of the fight.

Scratch waited for the crowd to disperse before starting the return journey to the beach. He'd learnt from bitter experience that there was always someone who wanted to throw a stone at him or beat him with a stick whenever he passed by. When all was quiet, he came out from beneath the seating, and zig-zagged his way between the rows of seats, sniffing out any edible litter that had been left behind. He settled close to the car parking area to chew on some scraps of fried chicken he'd rooted out from a rubbish bin, when the old man passed by in the company of the man he'd just fought and a pot-bellied man with a fat cigar in his mouth. The trio concealed themselves behind a small lorry as the fat man passed money to the others. The old man looked at the money in his hand and began to complain. The fat man pulled the cigar from his wet lips and nodded to the fighter, who promptly slapped the old man across the face and pushed him away. The two laughed as he stumbled and fell to the floor.

Scratch couldn't understand what was happening, little realising that the fight had been a set-up – surely this was the same old man that he'd just seen knock the young fighter out of the ring? Why didn't he do the same again?

The old man raised his hand toward them, fanning the notes in his hand for them to see. This time the fat man stepped forward and slapped him across the face, angry that the old man persisted in arguing with him. Scratch reacted instinctively. Who better to recognise a fellow under-dog than he? Running from cover with a speed that surprised himself, he sank his teeth into the fat man's leg, ripping the material apart as he pulled against his calf muscle. Then, placing himself between the old man and his two enemies, Scratch barked with all the ferocity he could muster and flashed what few remaining teeth he had. The two men separated, moving around either side of him until it became difficult for him to watch them both at the same time. His head snatched from left to right, watching to see who would make the first move against him. The fat man pulled up one of the fence posts from the ground, untied the rope attached to it and raised it above his head. Concentrating on the imminent attack, Scratch didn't see the fighter drop to a crouch and swing his leg sideways toward him. The blow hit him across the ribs, instantly knocking the wind from his lungs and rolling him over on to his side. His old body was slow to react as the stick smashed down upon his shoulder and the fighter ran forward to swing another kick at him.

The old man summoned a memory of youth into

himself and sprang forward, blocking the kick with his instep and somehow managing to loop his leg around his attacker's and trip him over. As he fell, a second kick caught the fighter across the nose, sending a spray of blood across his chest. Stunned, the fighter sat in the dirt, stifling the flow with his hand, allowing Scratch time to recover and re-launch his attack on the fat man. He leapt into the air, seizing in his jaw the arm that held the post and brought it to the ground. The fat man rolled in the dirt, screaming aloud as Scratch began to taste the saltiness of blood on his tongue. The old man called some words to him and pulled him away from his prey. Scratch released the arm and stood his ground, barking defiantly as the old man held on to him and the blood and excitement turned his saliva to foam. The fat man had a look of sheer horror on his face as he saw the glistening foam upon the dog's teeth and scrambled sideways in the dirt to distance himself from another attack. He pointed at the dog's mouth as the fighter joined him and together they turned and ran from the car park.

After taking a few moments to recover their breath, the two old timers sat alongside each other, licking their wounds. Lim had a swollen face, and Scratch, two cracked ribs.

'Thanks for your help, old dog,' said Lim, patting his head. 'Those bullies were cheating me out of my money.'

Scratch didn't understand the words, but knew that the tone was friendly, unlike the usual voices he heard.

'I guess I owe you a meal at least for your bravery. Come on home with me and I'll sort something out for you.'

Reassured that he meant no harm, Scratch followed, as Lim beckoned him on, hoping that he was not being foolhardy.

Lim led the way through the back streets to the edge of town with Scratch limping alongside him. Once at his wooden shack, they sat side by side on the porch as Scratch fed on the plate of leftover food that Lim had been keeping for his supper. Beneath the dim, yellow light of a street lamp, he could now see what a sickly body the animal had. With his bones pressing out against his blotchy, threadbare skin, he looked like a sack of sticks. Scratch recognised the look of disgust on Lim's face and cast his eyes down, ashamed of how he looked.

Lim laid a hand across the back of his new companion. 'You and I can be friends if you like,' he said quietly. 'I've got no-one and you look like you've got no-one either. What do you say?'

Scratch licked his hand, which Lim took to mean yes.

Scratch had fallen asleep now and his death-like stillness made Lim wonder about who would bury his own body when his time came in the not too distant future. His customers couldn't understand what he saw in the flea-bitten, old dog and berated him for not chasing it away. But Lim knew why he cared: because he and the dog were one and the same, old, exhausted and with no one to care if they should live or die. He reached into his bedside cabinet and took out the bottle of cheap, cure-all medicine he kept there. A mixture of warming oils that evaporated on rubbing into the skin, it gave the impression of having a beneficial effect simply by increasing blood flow through the area. He rubbed the oil into Scratch's temples and then along his stomach, chanting the same Buddhist prayer that his mother had used on him when he had been unwell as a child. Scratch opened an eye and whimpered, partly in response to the strange, tingling sensation on his skin, and partly in gratitude for the attentiveness given by the only other living creature to care about him. He lay on the bed with Lim's hand across his back, just as it had done on that first night. He felt safe and wanted, his stomach full and his best friend beside him. What more could he wish for?

He closed his eyes and fell asleep.

6

Living like a dog

It had been nearly two months since Donner's escape and his owner, Karl Eidmans, had given up all hope of ever finding him. His contract term completed, he would soon be flying home to Germany. It comforted him to think of his dog as dead, rather than out there somewhere, wandering lost and hungry or dying a slow death from disease and starvation. As it happened, Donner was suffering none of these things – though his pride had certainly taken a hefty blow.

To be born a beach dog and learn the skills of survival from day one is the easier option. In Donner's case, he was a Dobermann and the product of a cosseted lifestyle that required few of his natural instincts to survive. He had fed on the finest cuts of meat, topped up with vitamin supplements, and had received a vet's attention at the slightest sign of sickness. But now he was out of his element and was in the real world, struggling day by day to feed himself and constantly having to keep an eye on the competition that would steal what few scraps he might manage to find.

His mate, Cabbie, was a mongrel, but far better equipped to survive than he, for all his breeding. It didn't matter that Donner had the inherited genes of generations of guard dogs, here a dog was judged upon how he performed. Cabbie was tough and sinewy, with a nose that could rummage through a garbage pile and instantly identify the good scraps from the foul. Whereas Donner thought that everything smelt and tasted foul. While his nose would only turn up fruit skins and packaging, hers would find fatty trimmings and poultry carcasses. Whatever she found, she shared with him, which of course meant less for her. At first he would reject it then, realising there was no alternative, would swallow his pride and return to eat the little that she had left to one side for him. It had taken him several weeks of continuous hunger before realising that he had to eat what was available and that no magical plate of food was going to be laid before him as he had been used to.

On the night they had met, she had taken him back to the abandoned shell of a lorry in which she lived. All the windows in the cab had long since been broken but the roof kept the worst of the monsoon rains at bay. The bench seat had plenty of room for two and she enjoyed the company of a partner sleeping alongside her during the night. She had successfully avoided having a litter with any of the other beach dogs in her young life, but had been unable to resist the genetic attractions of Donner's muscular frame, pure white teeth and confident personality.

It had taken her a while to understand how inexperienced he was in the ways of food gathering, for it seemed obvious to her that a dog of his size must be an accomplished provider. At first he had just sat around, as though expecting his food to appear out of nowhere, not seeming to know that if you didn't go out looking for your food, you would starve. The few small scraps she had first shared with him were immediately gobbled down, while she savoured hers, making then last as long as possible. She would chew the bones at length, mixing her saliva with the marrow to produce a tasty gravy. Her tight, small stomach would churn its contents joyfully, while his groaned with the emptiness that the scraps of food failed to satisfy.

As the weeks had passed by, the other dogs slowly accepted them as a pair and would no longer disturb her with their advances for fear of his attack. They would always exercise caution in his presence, for he was the dog around whom a legend had grown as the guardian of the world beyond the fence. One or two had dared to challenge him at first, but his bulk and superior strength had soon seen them off with wounds that would scar to remind them of their foolishness.

Donner knew that he wasn't doing his share and in the absence of scavenging skills resorted to using his intimidating presence to steal food from the more successful, yet smaller beach dogs. But as the weeks passed by, they noticed his bulk decrease until his bones began to push out against his flesh just like theirs. His decline made them more inclined to challenge his thievery and defend their food. It seemed he had a reputation he didn't deserve. At the end of the day, it wasn't a question of who was the biggest or strongest, but who was the hungriest. An otherwise timid dog could summon up savage reserves of energy if the price was right. And the price was survival.

Donner's skin had begun to irritate him from the bite of sand flies and the sucking mouths of the leeches he picked up in the grass. No longer was there the loving hand of his master to burn them from him with a cigarette tip. The loss of blood had sapped his strength even further, and the rotten food he had eaten had given him diarrhoea, dehydrating him. In this condition it was pointless to fight, and so he became a shadow of Cabbie, copying her every move in the struggle to cope in this hostile environment.

Donner had two urges within him: the first was the loyalty of a dog to his master, and the second was his instinct to mate and be with his own kind. Despite the difficulties he was now experiencing, he had chosen the latter and the company of fellow dogs rather than that of humans. It was his canine urges that had caused him to escape in the first place, and it was those same urges that now kept him with Cabbie and the pups that daily grew larger within her. It was for those reasons that he never returned to the fence, despite the dreams he had at night of doing precisely that. Dreams that made his paws twitch and curl as he slept, imagining himself running once more at his master's side.

He was tired of being tired. No matter what he did or didn't eat, the lethargy persisted. He could only sleep for so many hours, after that the idleness of doing nothing demotivated him from ever getting up off the ground, so that he lay there in a half-conscious stupor that made him useless both to himself and to his mate. He wasn't doing his fair share and he knew it. The same thought had run through his mind a hundred times, but he just couldn't seem to snap out of it. It was as though he was expecting something from outside of him to give him the impetus. Something like his master's voice.

Cabbie, now heavily pregnant, returned exhausted from a day's scavenging, to present him with what little she had to spare, and found him exactly as she had left him. He was fast becoming a liability.

She sat alongside him, pretending to be doing nothing in particular, while secretly watching him, studying him and trying to understand what he was going through. He'd spent the last two evenings sitting upright beside the beach with his head held high and howling plaintively into the night air. Had he another mate somewhere, she wondered. He certainly wasn't the all powerful provider she had once thought him to be, and it made her doubtful about the wisdom of having allowed him to mate with her. What kind of a father would he make with an attitude like this? How could she possibly hope to feed so many mouths when she was already going without to provide for him? Tomorrow, she decided, she would force him to spend the whole day with her and rid him of his melancholy.

Next morning, Cabbie arose with the first rays of sun as they broke through the moving vegetation and flickered about the inside of the cab. She immediately set about prodding Donner's flanks with her nose. He stirred from his sleep and looked quizzically at her. She nuzzled him once more, lifting his rear legs from the bench seat and whimpered excitedly. Confused that anything so interesting could be happening at that time of day, he reluctantly raised himself to sitting and looked about himself, but saw nothing out of the ordinary. She pushed him from behind, forcing his front feet off the seat and through the open cab window into open space. He half fell, half leapt from the cab to the ground below only to be joined by her springing down alongside him. She ran around to his front, barking now to enthuse him to continue. Still unsure of what was happening, he followed her lead into the trees, wondering what could be so important as to necessitate all this fuss. She led off along one of the regular paths they used until they reached a smouldering fire of litter swept together by one of the hotel's night guards. From there she ducked into the bushes and hugged the wall until they reached a gateway. Donner's stomach began to rumble, voicing its displeasure at being disturbed so early in the day without having been filled the night before. He tasted the acid that rose in the back of his throat and hoped this effort was not going to

69

be in vain. Cabbie took a final glance about her and ran full speed across the open car park, to hide beneath one of the parked cars. As Donner settled down beside her, his nostrils caught the first whiff of her prey. Meat! Fresh, red, bloody meat.

Inside the kitchen, one of the staff was busy trimming the side of beef and deciding precisely how he would butcher it with the variety of knives, saws and cleavers that hung from the stainless steel bar in front of him. Preoccupied by the imaginary lines that his eyes traced around the animal's curves and joints, he didn't notice the two dogs push their sniffing noses through the rubber flap doors at the rear of the kitchen. From behind the sacks of vegetables, two pairs of eyes scanned the room. Apart from the butcher, there was no-one else to be seen. Cabbies's paw began to shiver nervously as she remembered the dead dogs she had seen with her own eyes, lying atop the garbage cans at the rear of the hotel. This hotel had a reputation of no second chance. No dog that she knew had ever stolen food from this place and lived to enjoy it. Those who had tried, had either never been seen again or graced the garbage can with a gaping wound in their body. Her plan was simple, but ruthless. Her litter to be took priority over all else, and with so little food, their growth inside her was already in jeopardy, let alone feeding them and their lazy father as well. This would either be the test that made him prove his worth, or one or both of them would be gracing the garbage can that day. He needed something to shake him up and needed a reward for doing so. What better reward than a choice cut of meat as heavy as a pup. If he succeeded, it could mean a fresh start, but if he failed then she would have one less burden to carry.

There were two trays on the wooden chopping block and two silver buckets on the floor into which the butcher placed various organs, trimmings and joints. The smell was torture for the two dogs as they sat impatiently behind the sacks, the saliva dripping from their gaping mouths. For once Donner was alert and beginning to feel like his old self. The adrenalin that now ran through his veins reminded him of times in the past when he had chased intruders from the agricultural station. Cabbie no longer needed to check with sidelong glances that her mate was alert and ready to strike, for now he was coming around her side, eager to be the first there. But she knew better than to launch themselves now, for all they would receive for risking their lives would be a mouthful of offal, so she shouldered Donner to one side, forcing him to retreat behind her for fear of being seen.

It was probably less than five minutes, but it seemed like hours before the butcher was finally slicing thick slabs of flesh from the rump of the carcass and stacking them into the tray alongside. When there were about five, he stopped, looked up at the array of tools before him and called aloud to the far end of the kitchen. There was no reply, so he called again, only louder. Still no reply. Cursing aloud, he walked away in search of the sharpening steel.

Cabbie edged forward, with Donner pressing upon her, anxious to communicate that he too thought that this was their moment. She waited until the two-leg was out of sight and sprang from hiding. In the buckets were liver and kidney which, although tempting, were not what she had her mind set upon. She stood on her hind legs and pulled one of the huge slabs of meat towards her. As it slid from the tray, it swung in her jaws, its weight immediately pulling her head down. It took her by surprise, for she had never felt such a weight of food in her jaws before. Beside her, Donner had been unable to resist the instant gratification of a mouthful of liver from the silver bucket that so reminded him of the food his master used to feed him with.

What was he doing? she thought to herself. This was no time to eat! The priority was to get away with something worthwhile and eat later. She butted his side until he withdrew his liver-stained face from the bucket and, seeing the dripping, red steak that swung from her jaws, he too reached for the tray above.

At the far end of the kitchen, the butcher gave the final few strokes of his blade either side of the sharpening steel, then reached to return it to its hook above. Suddenly a loud clatter came from his bench as the tray of meat fell to the floor. In his haste, Donner had pulled the tray with the meat until it had fallen, casting its contents on to the concrete floor. He grabbed at the largest steak, just as the sharpening steel completed a final spin through the air and struck him across the shoulder.

From the doorway, Cabbie looked back, startled by the clatter, only to see the rod bouncing off Donner's back. Run! she tried to call to him, but the steak in her mouth muffled her bark. What was he doing? Why didn't he snatch the meat and join her?

But Donner stood defiant, growling angrily and standing his ground as the butcher came closer, calling for help and waving his long bladed knife menacingly before him. This was Donner's natural instinct as a guard dog, to defend, whether it be his master, his home or himself; this was what his breed was meant to do. He enjoyed the rush of the moment as the blood surged within him and he felt the anticipation of a violent victory; a feeling that had been rare since his escape. The prize of meat was secondary now. Of prime concern was the defence of his position, of not backing up or giving in. The meat now left behind him, he advanced on the two-leg, his lips drawn back over his white fangs and his eyes fixed upon his attacker's. From deep within him came a growl that seemed to have originated in the darkest bowels of the earth, its resonance seeming to tremble the air between them, forcing the two-leg to freeze on the spot. Never before had the butcher experienced a dog so determined to fight. If his first stab failed, he could lose an arm. Was it worth it? With his first step backward and the lowering of the knife a mere three inches, his body language had conceded defeat, and Donner knew it. As the two-leg continued his retreat, so Donner back-stepped, his eyes never leaving his would-be attacker until he reached the tray, then, choosing the largest piece of meat, he glanced back to look for Cabbie. Her wide-eyed stare of amazement at his performance warmed his heart.

Continuing to back-step, he calmly passed after her through the doorway to safety.

Outside they stood encircled by four hotel staff alerted by the calls from within. The dogs glanced at each other, realising that escape would not be so easy after all. The four spaced themselves apart and reached for brooms, pieces of wood and old chairs to fight with, just as the swing doors to the kitchen burst violently open to reveal two screaming staff waving meat cleavers above their heads. The four were as stunned by this spectacle as the dogs themselves, and momentarily froze in disbelief. In that moment of confusion, the dogs bolted, between one pair of legs and around another, across the car park and in two different directions once past the gate. They ran, ducking into the vegetation at the first opportunity, but finding it difficult to breath with such large hunks of meat in their mouths. Slowing eventually to a walk, each made their way until the screaming voices behind them disappeared, before settling down to enjoy their reward. Donner tore at the flesh, anxiously gulping down chunks as though it were going to be taken away any moment, while Cabbie, as always, savoured hers, licking the blood lazily from both sides before chewing and sucking upon it at her leisure.

Scar, as his name implied, was a battle-scarred survivor of many a fight. And with that experience came the cunning of a dirty fighter. He had an attitude of stubborn perseverance that had earned him a reputation as a dog who never gives up. He would never back down from a fight, even if he knew he would lose, because he was confident that if he could inflict sufficient injury upon his adversary, he would ensure that he was never attacked again. But there was always an exception. He had been in the pack of dogs that moonlit night at the perimeter fence when Donner had joined them. The others had looked to him to lead the challenge, but he had not met it, believing, like they, that this was a devil dog and not only undefeatable but one who would kill rather than injure. He had once forced himself upon Cabbie when she was too young to bear his pups, then given up all hope when she chose the devil dog instead. Thereafter he had despised her and avoided the pair of them whenever their paths crossed. But he had noticed Donner's physical decline and wondered whether the time was approaching when his defeat could win back Cabbie. Jealousy was a powerful motive.

Scar knew that there was food nearby and good food too. This smell wasn't the putrid type that he was used to, but quite the opposite, the rare smell of fresh, raw meat. He followed the scent away from the road and up through the forest until he heard a rustling amongst the leaves and twigs ahead of him.

Cabbie lay with her head to one side, pulling on the meat held between her paws and oblivious to the danger that approached. Not until Scar was standing a yard behind her, did she look back and feel her heart jump within her chest. He looked at her with a mixed expression that she found hard to read. His confusion about wanting her, despising her and the need to eat, all sent conflicting signals of his intent. She pulled herself forward, covering the meat with her chest and hoping he had not seen it, while remaining passive and unchallenging on the earth before him. He approached and began smelling her, hesitantly at first, then more freely as he realised she didn't resist as she had done in the past. Forgetting for the moment the smell of food that had brought him there, he allowed her scent to remind him of the one time he had unsuccessfully forced her to mate with him, but as he closed toward her head the smell of fresh meat on her breath brought him back to the present. Now she read his eyes clearly, for his thoughts were once again focused. The look told her to surrender her food or fight for it. She opened her mouth to show there was no more, but the warmth of her body sent a flood of unmistakable scent signals from the steak beneath her that no dog could miss. He growled for her to move, but she resisted, forcing him to push his nose beneath her side to confirm what his nose had told him. She couldn't risk losing such a prize and bit his exposed ear, causing him to snatch away. As he withdrew she pulled the meat from beneath her and ran. Seeing it now, he fell upon her hind quarters, knocking her back legs away with a practised sweep of his front paw and sinking his teeth into the edge of her thigh. She fell yelping into the dirt, but holding on to the meat in her mouth. He shook her thigh so that his teeth tore into her, but she refused to release it. Climbing over her prostrate body, he fell forward, seized one end of the meat and began a tug of war, punctuated by muffled growls as they argued over ownership. Bringing his right paw around, he pushed the side of her face, digging his claws into her lips until the blood ran. Little by little, Cabbie could feel the threads of flesh tear away from between her teeth as the stronger dog gradually pulled the meat from her mouth. She whined aloud, pleading for him to share it, but was ignored.

With the fullest stomach he had had in months, Donner cautiously retraced his steps towards the hotel gate and, once satisfied that the two-legs were not in hiding, set off in search of his mate. The scent of fresh meat that he followed became obscured as the path of another dog, who had recently passed urine on the track, overpowered his nostrils. As he circled the spot, he heard the whine of Cabbie in the distance. Perhaps the two-legs had found her? he thought. How could he have been so stupid as to have eaten his meat before checking she was okay? Disregarding the direction of the scent trail, he ran at full speed towards her call with the excitement of his earlier defence still within him. Cabbie's trick had worked. He felt like a new dog.

The outer edge of the meat was all that remained in Cabbie's mouth when Donner launched himself into the air and slammed his body weight into Scar's shoulder. Forgetting the meat torn from his mouth, Scar rolled skilfully over in the dirt and back on to his feet to face his attacker. Had it been any other dog, he would have launched his counter-attack regardless, but the sight of Donner flashed his memory back to the night at the fence and the fear he had then felt. That moment's hesitation was all that Donner needed, as his gaping mouth closed over Scar's, slamming his jaw shut and allowing his own teeth to punch through his lips on to solid gum. They rolled over and over, their back legs kicking into each other's abdomens until Scar, laying upon his back, froze and fought no more. His head dropped back and his vulnerable throat was exposed in surrender. The submissive gesture was recognised by Donner but not trusted, for he had seen Scar use this trick before. If he were to let go now, Scar would feign defeat, turn away, then re-attack from behind by going for his testicles. Instead, he held his grip, stared down into his opponent's eyes and used the same resonant growl that had made the butcher retreat. The message was clear – he knew the trick.

Scar read the eyes and urinated with fear. The Dog from Hell would kill him if he dared to try it. He remained limp until the jaws released him and for the first time in his life whimpered for forgiveness. Donner stood firm as his opponent crouched away across several yards of open ground, before finally standing and turning tail to run off into the trees and lick a fresh set of scars. But, even as he left, Scar was busy thinking of how he could take his revenge.

7

One parent family

The dilemma that now faced Catcher was how she could leave the pups unattended while she went scavenging for food. With no mate to share the parenting, her workload was doubled, and the time spent away from the den only made her anxious about what might be happening in her absence. How could she trust them to stay inside when they were at that exploratory age and curious to learn about everything around them?

It was the first day after Bouncer's death and if they were to eat, she would have to leave them alone while she went scavenging. She waited outside, hiding in the nearby bushes to see who would be the first to come out. As expected, it was Snarl who took it upon himself to be the first in everything. She waited until he had committed himself and was fully out in the open, then descended upon him, knocking him sideways into the ground and biting his hind-quarters with a firmness that left the screaming pup in no doubt that this was his one and only warning. She returned him, firmly clasped between her jaws, then as a warning to the others, tossed him unceremoniously to one side. He sat there, his tail tucked between his legs, shaking in nervous anticipation of what might follow, much to the amusement of the others, who were pleased to see him put in his place. For the next two days, before she left, she repeated the waiting process, but neither Snarl nor any of the others dared show themselves.

Food was, as always, hard to find, but at least she had the advantage of only four mouths to feed now that the youngest had been cast out. She refused to think about her, except to confirm in her mind that if not dead already, she soon would be.

Today would be a particularly difficult day for Catcher, for today was the day when the tourists departed in large groups to visit the temples and waterfall. It was an all-day trip that included meals, allowing the hotels and restaurants to give many of their staff a day off. Catcher roamed from one stretch of beach to another, but there were no scraps to be found or begged for. Everywhere she went, she came across other beach dogs similarly wandering with the same despondent look in their eyes. The competition was intense, causing ill-tempered fights to break out here and there as rivals squabbled over what little there was. Catcher knew she couldn't risk injury and, keeping well out of the way of the others, remained hungry.

The patrol dogs especially enjoyed days like this. A favourite trick of theirs was to wander down to the empty beach with a bone from the kitchen and discard it conspicuously in the sand, as though their hunger had been satisfied. They would then settle down in the shade about twenty yards away and see which beach dog would be fool enough, or hungry enough, to take the bait. It was the canine version of fishing. Presently a group of beach dogs would gather around the perimeter and stare longingly at the bone, imagining how perfectly it would fit between their jaws, how succulent the shreds of meat would be and how much marrow they would suck from its interior. The patrol dog would allow them to crawl forward, pretending not to see their gradual incursion, then suddenly jump to attention, stare straight at them and intimidate them into retreat. What satisfaction it gave them to watch these beggars suffer in the heat.

Today, it was Catcher who, in desperation, dared to creep towards the bait. Sultan, the patrol dog that guarded the Blue Lagoon Hotel, had earned himself a reputation as one of the most vicious on the beach. A mongrel himself, he had been adopted by the hotelier for the simple reason that Sultan was a bully. Unlike Donner, who simply did his job without inflicting any more pain than necessary, Sultan took great pleasure in causing suffering. It mattered not at all to him that they were his own kind, for he had only one loyalty – to the hand that fed him.

Catcher pretended to be dozing in the hot sun, while

Sultan pretended not to see her. Her persistence was rewarded only with the gradual disappearance of the other dogs that lingered nearby, as one by one they each tired of ever winning the prize. Could she really smell the bone at that distance or was it her imagination getting the better of her? Whatever, the saliva ran about her mouth just the same. She looked in its direction one more time, as casually as she could, as though looking beyond it to something in the distance that was far more interesting, then used her peripheral vision to check on his readiness to strike. He seemed to be looking towards the hotel, as though something was catching his attention. It was now or never.

The driver slapped his hand against the metal side of the truck for a second time and called again to his dog. 'Come on, Sultan. Let's go!'

Sultan was hesitant, torn between a ride into town and tormenting the beach dogs. He certainly didn't want to leave a free meal on the beach, but the insistent tone of his master's voice allowed him no leeway; he had to obey.

Catcher waited until the dog had leapt into the rear of the truck, then made her move. Summoning up what little energy she had, she bolted across the sand toward the bone.

From the back of the truck, Sultan saw her and instinctively leapt over the tailgate and bounded away in pursuit.

A clean snatch of the bone between her teeth and Catcher was away, heading for the tangle of shrubs that bordered the beach. Less than thirty yards back, Sultan was gaining on her. But there was another in the chase, for bringing up the rear was the hotelier, swinging a bamboo stick above his head and calling after his disobedient animal. The gap was closing between the two dogs, so that as Catcher smashed through the shrubbery, Sultan was practically upon her. She immediately swerved to her left to avoid the fallen tree she knew was there, but he thudded into it with a startled yelp. As she weaved her way through the tangle of undergrowth, she heard yet more yelps of pain as the hotelier repeatedly struck his dog with the cane, hurling abuse at him for running away when he had called.

Catcher, now safe from pursuit, stopped to catch her breath and examine her reward. She had made an enemy today, a bad enemy who would remember her and the beating she had caused, but at least today her pups would eat.

She returned home exhausted, but her efforts had not gone unrewarded. The threads of meat that clung to the bone would scarcely satisfy the pups, so she would have to chew up the bone for their young teeth and share what would normally have been hers alone. They welcomed her with eager anticipation of the meal they trusted her to provide and gathered excitedly around, licking at the protruding ends of the bone that jutted from either side of her mouth. As she set the bone down, she counted them, then after looking around to double check, realised the worst – Snarl was missing.

She left the pups pulling the bone to and fro between

them and scrambled back into the failing daylight. She called out into the early evening, once in each direction, pausing in between to listen for any response. But there was none. She called again, louder this time, realising that Snarl must have wandered further afield. Where would he have gone? she thought to herself as she conjured up a mental image of every route she had taught them. Clearly the pup hadn't learnt his lesson from the teeth marks she had left in his thigh. The problem now was how could she trust the others to remain there while she went to look for him? If only Bouncer had been there to help, this would never have happened and she allowed herself to momentarily recall the image of her youngest licking at her dead father's mouth.

She returned to the den to distract herself from such thoughts and watched the remains of her dwindling family push and shove each other around the bone. By the time the beam of light that poured in through the entrance had faded into the shadows of the night, the meal had been finished and the pups lay sleeping together in a tangled mess. Now that it was safe to leave them, she crept quietly out into the warm night air and searched a few hundred yards in each direction, calling woefully for her lost pup, but there was only one response, that of a lonely male looking for a mate. She returned in the early hours of the morning, finally resolved to the fact that Snarl was either dead or lost beyond the range of her call.

At first light, while the others were still sleeping, she set off for the only place she could imagine he would want to return to – the stretch of road where his father had died. Even before she reached the spot, she knew she was close from the stench that carried in the air. Coming out of the undergrowth, it saddened her to see no trace of Snarl beside what remained of Bouncer after the animals of the night had taken their share. As she recalled some of the happy times they had spent together, it was hard to believe that this flattened, insect-covered mound was once flesh and blood with character and vitality. She remembered their meeting at the rock pool and how gentle he had been with the pups. The memories just underlined how lonely she felt and, overcome, she had to leave.

Snarl was convinced that he could hunt better than the rest of the litter and possibly as well as some of the adults he had seen. He knew that his mother had been spending longer and longer periods away from the den and bringing home barely enough for them, let alone herself. He decided that it was time he helped. After all, he was the eldest.

Having set out in the early evening of the day before, he had wandered from scent to scent and path to path until it all ended up in a confused mess. Unable to find any food, he soon tired and, with darkness closing around him, gave up trying to find his way home and curled up beneath a bush.

Next morning he was awoken before first light by the grumbling complaint of his empty stomach. During the night he'd missed the company of his brothers and sisters about him and felt vulnerable for the first time in his short life. He set off toward the sound of clattering metal, thinking that where there was activity, there would be two-legs, and where they were, there was always food. He arrived at the service road of one of the larger hotels and peered through the clouds of swirling diesel fumes as a tipper truck finished emptying the last of the commercial sized wastebins. Nearby a dilapidated bus was discharging the kitchen workers who had been brought in from the nearby villages. In single file, they climbed the concrete steps besides the loading bay, where farmers were unloading their produce on to trolleys that kitchen porters trundled inside. Snarl was curious about so much activity and there was no mistaking the waft of food that escaped every time a porter took a crate of vegetables through the swing doors to the kitchen.

He waited until the crowd dispersed, then edged his way forward, passing beneath the farmer's truck and climbing the now empty steps that led to the alluring smells. Watching carefully and timing the to-ing and fro-ing through the swing doors, he waited for his chance and neatly followed on the heels of a porter into the kitchen. From beneath a stainless steel table, he looked out at the ankle height world of moving feet and wondered what his father would have done in such a situation.

He lay there on his belly for what seemed an eternity. Behind him the double doors had stopped swinging open and shut, effectively trapping him in the kitchen. The only consolation was the reassuring smell of food nearby. The noises about him were all new and strange, from the squeak of rubber shoes on polished tiles to the whirr and grind of a meat slicer vibrating down through the table above him. Being so very much out of his element, he was vulnerable and he knew it. Moving away from the feet that shuffled perilously close to him, he looked toward the other side of the kitchen and saw a large, shining door open up, leading to a room from which a two-leg carried a dangling handful of dead chickens by their legs. How clever he was to find a place where he could find enough food for his entire family. My mother will be so proud of me, he thought to himself.

Passing from beneath one table to another, he was now only yards away from the door. A final look around and he was in. The strangest of sensations occurred as he entered. A chill of cold air, like nothing he had experienced before, fell about his shoulders and descended, clingingly, down to his feet. The sudden change of temperature almost sucked the breath from his tiny lungs, and stopped him in his tracks as though he'd reached some invisible barrier. His instincts told him to retreat, but his hunger and need to prove himself drove him on. Here and there were wooden crates, stuffed with green plants that were strangely devoid of scent, while above hung featherless chickens, their ankles hooked to shiny metal bars. Ahead, a heavy, plastic curtain hung across his path, separating him from the next section. As he pushed his nose through, a coldness far more intense than before chilled the dampness of his nose. Up until now in his short life, he had known only heat and more heat; the concept of cold was beyond his comprehension. The dangers of the hotel's deep freeze unit was something that his lifestyle could never have prepared him to face.

The pads of his feet began to tingle as he edged gingerly forward across the frosted, white floor and into the white mist that cascaded down from the machinery clanking noisily above. Before him stood stacks of what looked like meat dusted in white powder. As his warm tongue passed over its icy surface, it stuck fast. The shock sent him reeling backwards, almost tearing his tongue from his mouth before it came free. What kind of meat was this, he wondered? Meat that bites you back? As he cast his eyes about him for an easier target, a gust of air swirled about him, followed by the cushioned slam of the airtight door and total darkness. The refrigerator had been shut.

Entombed in a world of sensations beyond anything he had known, he remained motionless. Within the darkness the cold seemed to penetrate even deeper, biting through his thin flesh until it chilled the bone and caused his limbs to tremble uncontrollably. He tried to imagine what his father would have done in the same circumstances and began to sniff the air for a scent to follow, but succeeded only in chilling his nostrils with the icy air. As numbness set into his extremities, he began to feel tired, with an overwhelming urge to curl up into a tight ball and sleep until the cold night had passed and the morning sun shone once again. Pushing his nose into the darkness he brushed by a freshly hung string of sausages and toyed with them for a moment as they swung either side of his head. He bit into one, hoping it was food but felt only a cold hardness with the vaguest taste of meat within. Still it was better than nothing, so he pulled it free, curled up on the floor and chewed upon its end. Each morsel that eventually tore free slid uneasily down to his stomach, chilling his insides as it went. Occasionally his paw would brush against his nose, yet he could feel no contact between the two as the numbness spread. A few minutes later and his jaw began to ache, as though he'd been chewing the whole day long. An overwhelming tiredness that was impossible to resist pulled his eyelids down, once, twice and then held them shut, darkness within the darkness, as sleep took a hold. No longer aware of the numbing pain in his limbs, he lay curled in a semi circle with the end of the string of sausages trailing from his mouth.

When Snarl had not returned home by the second day, Catcher knew that he was dead. With only three of her five pups left and no mate to help her, she knew that this den was no longer safe for them. She would have to find them a new home, away from the dangers that surrounded them here. A place where she could leave the pups unattended without having to worry while she searched for food. That meant going to the far end of the beach, to the ABC huts. The food was more scarce there, so she would have to make the long journey back and forth several times a day, but at least their chances of survival would be greater there.

8

Teach an old dog

It had taken Scratch another two days of sleeping in the shade of Lim's shack before the bug was finally out of his system. Periodically, the old man would come to check on his progress, to leave scraps of food and speak words of reassurance. Unpleasant as it was, he cleared away the trails of diarrhoea and washed Scratch down with a sponge and water every evening. Lim had been there for him when he needed it most and Scratch would never forget that. Perhaps one day it would be his turn to repay the kindness. On the morning of the third day he was gone. Departing as he had arrived – without notice. He was sure Lim would understand.

Returning to the more familiar haunts of the beach, Scratch set out to search the shoreline for any debris that may have washed up. Many years ago he had found a goat that must have fallen from some passing ship, and although such a find had never been repeated, he never gave up hope of finding another such prize. But there was nothing except for the occasional piece of driftwood or coconut to be found.

Leaving the beach, he worked his way along the edge of the mangrove swamp toward the lagoon beyond. The mangrove was home to strange, slithering creatures, their sliminess making them all the more difficult to catch as they slid away into the muddy tangle of roots and sucking mud that was their home. So unpleasant was their taste, that the dogs would only hunt them when all else had failed.

Coming out of the far side of the mangrove, he followed the well-worn path that led alongside the lagoon to the village nearby. Halfway there he picked up the scent of another dog and, always preferring to be cautious, side-stepped into the tall grass alongside the path and paused for a while. But no other dog passed by. He began to push ahead when a whimpering sound came from deeper within the grass. It was a sound he knew all too well – the sound of another dog in distress. Cautiously edging forward towards the sound, he came upon an old car tyre, lying on its side in an area of trodden down grass where the village children had been playing. The noise was coming from within the tyre but there was no dog to be seen. Curiosity getting the better of him, Scratch approached and peered over the edge to see a thin, bedraggled pup curled up at its centre. At once he spotted the hardened crust that had formed over the pup's eye and instinctively knew that it had come there to die. But what did he care? Life was tough and when he'd nearly died himself just a few days ago, no dog had given him any help.

The pup hadn't even noticed his arrival, let alone his departure, and simply lay there, comforting itself by sucking on the end of its tail and whimpering. For the past two weeks she had valiantly tried to survive by living on the slimy creatures in the mangrove. Alone and unwanted, she'd now lost the will to persevere and found in sleep the only comfort remaining.

Scratch had taken but a few paces beyond the clearing when the whimpering stopped. He paused, listening for its return, but none came. As the silence continued he realised that the pup had died within those few seconds. Suddenly feeling guilty for not helping, he lowered his head in shame. Better, he thought, that his old body should have died and this youngster should have lived. What need had he of yet another day of uncertainty and loneliness? Turning around, he returned to the clearing and looked down at the still body in the tyre. It looked too small to be out on its own, and Scratch assumed the parents must have been killed. As he smelled its body and looked closer at the damaged eye, he felt the faintest blow of warm air on to his nose and realised the pup was still breathing. He reached forward with one paw and dragged at the pup's shoulder until it raised its head and turned its good eye towards him. Thankful for having been given a second chance, Scratch decided then and there to take the youngster into his care. After all, if a two-leg could do it for him, surely he could do the same for a fellow dog.

The pup rose to its feet and, without resisting, allowed Scratch to complete his examination of her. The first priority, Scratch decided, was some food, followed by a good look at the infected eye. But he couldn't trust the pup to stay put while he went to scavenge, and so nudged the pup out of the tyre, encouraging her to follow him. She didn't resist, and stumbled clumsily along behind him, grateful to be in the company of her own kind once again.

Every so often, Scratch would have to stop to allow the weak youngster to catch up, until after a mile or so they arrived at the outskirts of the village. Ever mindful of danger, Scratch pushed the pup into the undergrowth while he went ahead to explore. Making his way along the back of some huts, he crept stealthily with ears raised and nostrils flaring to catch any hint of danger or food. He stopped alongside a hut where an old lady squatted beside a griddle of fish, fanning the flames from a pile of coconut husks beneath. Scratch's years of experience automatically took over. He lay low, as low as possible, and waited for his moment to come. Some five minutes passed before his patience was rewarded by the cry of a baby from within the hut. Quickly stuffing the last of the husks into the fire, the old lady hurried inside, leaving the food unguarded. Swiftly and silently seizing the moment, Scratch ran forward and, using only the tip of his paw, knocked one of the dozen or so fish from the edge of the griddle and on to the ground. Picking it up with his teeth – his lips retracted away from the hot flesh – he ran for cover. Of course he could have taken several fish, or the biggest fish in the centre of the griddle, but no, wise old Scratch knew from experience that such a theft would be noticed and the villagers would be all the more on their guard next time. Better to have a small fish every so often than a single, fat fish only once.

Pushing his way back into the undergrowth, he presented his prize to the patient pup who fell eagerly upon the succulent flesh. As he looked on, strange emotions arose within him; emotions that he had never known before. He felt a pride in being the provider for one so tiny; protective for one so inexperienced; and – for the first time in his life – a sense of having a purpose, for until now his lonely life had been devoted only to self-preservation. Blighted from his youth with physical handicaps, he had fathered no litters and shared little company with the other beach dogs, who shunned him. Now, at a time in his life when old age had made him feel even less worthwhile, he was being given the opportunity to think about the welfare of someone other than himself . . . and he liked it. As he watched the orphan feed, he realised the wealth of experience he could pass on to her.

Once all the flesh had been torn from the bone, Scratch pushed the pup aside and took the head and bones for his share. Then, settling down alongside her, set about licking the perimeter of the infected eye. The pup didn't resist, seeming to understand that Scratch was trying to help, and innocently curled up against the mottled, pink skin that so disgusted the other dogs.

* * *

Four weeks of rapid learning followed, during which Crusty's once prominent ribs became hidden beneath a fresh layer of puppy fat. Crusty was the obvious name for her because of the persistent discharge that dried around her now opaque eye. Her strength improved day by day, and the plump stomach that now hung beneath her was testimony to the skill and cunning of her mentor. As a provider of food, Scratch had surpassed the combined efforts of both Crusty's natural parents.

The one thing that she found difficult to understand was why they had turned inland and moved away from the company of the other beach dogs. Scratch had led her along paths and tracks that wandered far from the salty smell of the sea. There were two reasons: the first was that Scratch now thought of her as his own and was cautious of showing her off to the other dogs until he had further cemented the bond between them. He had a dread of losing her and his new found purpose in life. The second reason related to their destination.

There followed a journey of discovery for a pup who'd previously known only two directions away from her home: the one that led to the lagoon and the one that led to the road where tragedy had occurred so early in her life. She avoided remembering the event by distracting herself with the fascinating world that Scratch revealed all around her. Scenery changed from wide, curving vistas of land meeting endless sea to walls of dense, tangled vegetation that at times seemed as though it was trying to close in and swallow them up. Her ears retuned to a new variety of sounds. Gone was the relentless wash of waves upon the beach, the wind that vibrated the humming palm fronds overhead and above all the call of dog to dog. Here there was birdsong by day and insect chorus by night, and a stillness in the air that made it seem warmer the further from the sea they travelled. Every day there was a new lesson to be learned and every place they visited presented more opportunities for Scratch to demonstrate his versatility at finding food.

She soon learned the routine of 'wait and see' that he used whenever an opportunity arose to demonstrate some new aspect of finding, stealing or begging for food. He would settle her down at a safe location nearby to watch him in action. Sometimes he failed, but mostly he succeeded, to the point where at times she was so bloated that her small but growing stomach could take no more. In his enthusiasm for his new lease of life, Scratch was surpassing himself. Each day would end with what had become a ritual of him cleaning her eye, and she in turn would groom his hairless skin with her tongue, not understanding why his body was so different from her parents and caring even less.

They had now reached the edge of a palm oil plantation and from the expectant stare with which Scratch studied the plantation manager's bungalow, she realised that they were at journey's end. As they settled for the night beneath a bush, she wondered what surprise the following day would bring.

At first light Scratch awoke her and led the way along the perimeter fence to the double gates that led to the bungalow. She stumbled, sleepy-eyed at first until he slowed near the gate in the compound wall and looked hesitantly through the wrought ironwork. Now fully awake, she brimmed with curiosity at what it could be that had brought them on such a long journey.

Within the compound the guard dog stood alert. Short and rounded with a bushy brown coat, he had the friendly appearance of a family pet rather than the guard dog whose duties he was performing. He heard no sound, smelt no scent, yet his sixth sense warned him of an approaching intruder. He moved toward the gate, stopping short of it and stood his ground.

Crusty could smell him, but the breeze on her nose told her that her own was being carried away behind her. Yet still the guard dog knew of their presence and swivelled its ears, seeking out any sounds. Crusty watched on in absolute silence, fascinated by the stand-off and curious as to how the guard dog couldn't see them standing no more than five yards away. Why didn't he bark? Was he so unsure of their presence?

The guard dog began to advance, sweeping its head from side to side like a radar scanner, until coming closer still, he began rolling his lips back over his teeth and growled at the intruders. As he moved closer, Crusty could see that his eyes were white and glazed. He was blind!

With a stealth acquired from years of stealing, Scratch silently reverse-stepped away from the gate with Crusty trying clumsily to copy him, until they were twenty feet away. He then turned casually away to return along the path with the pup following behind. This had been merely an introduction, there would be many opportunities over the following days to observe this guard dog in action, but first they needed some food.

Scratch had discovered the blind dog several years ago during one of his occasional forays away from the beach during the rainy season when food was scarce. Of course, he didn't know how the dog had become blind, but he knew that a one-eyed pup could learn many lessons from observing such an animal.

The guard dog returned to his kennel, just inside the gates and settled down on the sack-covered floor. He knew there had been another dog nearby, his instincts told him that, but why hadn't the other dog barked at his approach? Why did it just stand there watching him? And why did the breathing he had heard sound like an old dog when the footsteps had been those of a pup? Something unusual was happening and he was determined to find out.

He had been given to the estate manager, Kucha, as a pup by one of the tractor drivers who discovered the litter in his fertiliser hopper. Or perhaps it was more accurate to say what remained of the litter after the spreader unit had been turned on. The pup soon became the constant companion and playmate of his two young sons. Wherever the children were, so too would be the pup, making sure he was involved in whatever activity they were.

It had been on a particularly hot afternoon when the children were sailing paper boats in the open drain at the back of the kitchen that it happened. The two boats raced side by side along the gully as the children ran to the end to catch them before they fell into the water trap. They shrieked excitedly as each boat snagged and spun, taking turns to be in the lead as they drifted toward the children's waiting hands. So engrossed were they that they hadn't noticed the jet black body that slithered through the grass beside the drain, then rose vertically to stare with its needle point, red eyes into their faces. Instant silence befell them as their hands froze in mid air and the boats sailed silently by. So many times they had been lectured about snakes by their father and at school, but now that the hypnotic stare had taken hold of them, their memories became vacant. But their playmate did react and placed himself between the children and the snake, returning the fixed stare and giving a series of defiant barks. The snake began to vibrate and leaned its curving body menacingly close to the pup. The repeated sharpness of the bark caught the attention of one of the farmhands who, seeing the danger, called the children to him. But the pup remained, unwilling to drop his guard until he knew they were safe. Disregarding the farmhand's calls, he continued to stare down the snake until one of the children called him. Instinctively, he dropped his guard and turning his head to the call, realised his error too late. He turned back just as the snake flicked its head forward and spat its venom into his eyes.

By the time they'd washed his burning eyes under the tap it was already too late. When they took him to the plantation clinic, the Matron simply volunteered to put him down. 'After all,' she said, 'what use is a blind dog to anyone?'

But she was wrong.

Kucha was a family man and believed that death was no reward for the brave little pup that had saved the lives of his children. And so the pup became an integral member of his family. As he grew to adulthood, so he progressively acquired the sixth sense possessed of all blind creatures. His hearing became fine-tuned, able to distinguish the minutest of variations in sound and to judge distance by the echo of his own bark. In time he learnt to identify every member of the estate not only by smell but by the way they breathed, walked or spoke. His favourite game was when the children tried to creep up on him from different directions and score points by touching him before he could turn to face them. He invariably won. Whenever visitors arrived at the gate, he would be introduced to them by his master and allowed to familiarise himself with their particular traits of sound and smell. These then became the equivalent of a password that would allow them to enter as a friend or be challenged as a foe. Stored within his memory was a catalogue of identifying features and only those people who matched his record were allowed inside the perimeter wall of the bungalow. Visitors arriving in groups were constantly amazed at how he determined who should wait outside and who could enter. To try and sidestep him was an invitation to being bitten and chased.

It was just such displays of skill as this that Crusty witnessed with Scratch over the following days. Keeping their distance, they would marvel at his ability to avoid obstacles in his path, gauging their size, distance and density by the penetration and reflection of his bark. Copying him, Crusty would close her good eye and practise wandering through the forest, barking every other stride for ten strides, twenty strides, and more, while Scratch looked on approvingly, pleased by her progress.

After two days of observation, he thought it would be interesting to introduce them to each other and led Crusty back along the path to the bungalow.

It had been about two years ago that Scratch had first met the blind dog himself and he hoped that he would be greeted as an old friend rather than as a trespasser. It had all begun during one of his inland trips when he had feigned injury at the side of the plantation road, hoping that the passing vehicle would take pity upon him and give him some food. Kucha had stopped to examine the apparently injured dog and sure enough offered the contents of his lunch box to him. The blind dog that accompanied him was naturally curious and sniffed Scratch cautiously. Concerned by the appearance of the hairless dog and fearing that he was near to death, Kucha loaded him on to the rear of the truck and took him home. Scratch stayed with them for two weeks, being fed and – because of his skin – having to suffer the indignity of being hosed down in the yard once a day. But during that time he had come to marvel at the abilities of the blind dog and established the beginnings of a friendship based on their relative handicaps.

The blind dog had spent the last two days running through the storehouse of smells by which he recognised friend and foe. Yet despite his inability to identify the scent that continued to carry on the wind, he knew that it wasn't a stranger. And when Scratch approached the gate on the third day, the strength of his scent now close by finally triggered the memory and he recalled the event of two years ago. But there was one other thing that he needed to clarify as well – the confusion he had experienced about the lightness of the footsteps. Each stood in hesitant silence, a yard away from either side of the gate, until at last Scratch barked an announcement of his presence, followed by the copycat yelp of Crusty. The blind dog responded and slid his nose against the gap in the fence. As he drank in the now remembered scent, he wondered what had brought the dog with no hair back to the estate. Unable to reach each other, they settled on either side of the gate until an hour later when the crunching of gravel under foot announced Kucha's return.

At first, he too was puzzled by the sight of the flea-bitten, buck-toothed dog and his fat-bellied, one-eyed friend. But reassured by his own dog's judgement at not barking at them, he crouched and offered a hand toward them as he too remembered the bald dog that had collapsed beside the road. A dog like Scratch was not easily forgotten.

Swinging open the compound gate for them, the dogs finally met and circled excitedly around each other. Scratch pushed the pup forward, who obediently allowed the blind dog to examine her. Sniffing closely around her body, he probed here and there with his nose; feeling the swell of her belly and the freshness of her young breath with no bad teeth. But when he reached the head, he detected the smell of her eye and ran a cautious tongue across its bulging lid. He now understood. This was his friend's blind pup and he wanted help.

Not knowing how much practice the pup had already put in during the past two days, the progress seemed impressive. The trio stayed together over the next two weeks, their time split between daytime games of tag with the children – in which Crusty would close her good eye – and hide and seek by night – where sight was of minimal advantage. Crusty soon mastered the basics of the 'echo bark' but needed more practice with her listening skills. She needed to learn to be so still that she could hear the breath passing within her own body, before she could hear the breath of another.

The final morning came when there was no more to learn. From now on she needed only to practise until it became second nature. The experience had been not so much 'teaching an old dog new tricks' as 'teaching a young dog old tricks'. As the dogs parted company that day, Scratch walked with deliberation, for he was now enthused about life and his new sense of purpose in bringing up his charge. As for Crusty, she bore little resemblance to that pitiful, helpless pup of only two months ago. She was now confident and skilled. Her mother would have been proud of her.

9

Home sweet home

In the three months since his escape, Donner had lost nearly half of his body weight. His initial failure at finding enough food to eat had been overcome not only as a result of the ego-building kitchen raid, but also by the fact that Cabbie had now produced a litter of six pups. This was a significant event in his life, for it now meant that he would have to give up any lingering thoughts he had about returning to his master. Now, not only did he have to maintain the momentum, but he had to increase his success rate if his pups were to grow to be fit and healthy. Their mixed parentage was the norm amongst beach dogs, yet Donner's genes clearly dominated in their physical appearance. No one who saw them could doubt that they were the closest thing to a Dobermann that Chaweng had ever seen. Whether Cabbie's genes would dominate in any other respect would be left for time to tell.

Cabbie had, naturally enough, chosen the cab of the truck as the birthplace for her first litter and lay curled around them on the bench seat, a patient and attentive mother. Despite the heat of the sun on the burning metal cab that surrounded them, she felt safer in the lorry than outside. Perhaps it was something to do with the sturdiness of its structure that provided a barrier between her and the harsh world in which they lived. But her sense of security was ill-founded, for the village children were very inventive when it came to playing. They could turn the rubbish heaps and cast-offs that littered the area into toys that would amuse them for hours on end. Tin cans, car tyres, empty sacks, wooden fruit crates, all provided the raw materials for their amusement. And so of course the lorry was their playground too. This hadn't been a problem when Cabbie only spent her nights there, but now that she had her litter, she would spend most of the day there too.

The lorry had been thoroughly stripped over the years that it had lain there, slowly disintegrating into the soil. Every engine part, bulb or length of electric cable that could be salvaged had been, leaving only a rusting hulk propped up on bricks. Its engine had been recycled, its tyres cut up into 'thousand milers' – the rubber sandals worn by the poor – and its cables burnt down to a puddle of molten plastic for their copper content. Yet, despite its appearance, the wreck remained a popular playground for the children. They would make imaginary journeys delivering produce far and wide, pretend it was a tank fighting a jungle war or a rocket ship flying to the stars. They would fight for control of the steering wheel and have competitions to see who could slam the door the hardest. They had broken every piece of glass or plastic they could find and squabbled over the remnants of shattered mirror to play signalling games with flashes of reflected sunlight. And, every evening, long after they had fallen asleep back in the village, Cabbie had moved through the shadows and returned to her ramshackle home.

But all that had changed now, for Cabbie was in residence and defended her home vociferously whenever they approached. So they devised a new game: firing stones at the wreck with catapults made from rubber inner tubes, and goading the dog to bark all the more. Like all children, they had a strange fascination with cruelty and teasing animals, and derived great pleasure from scoring a hit through the open cab windows. Had they behaved in such a way with their own kind, they would have surely been punished, but with a dumb animal and away from home there was no-one to rebuke them. Finally, Cabbie reached the end of her tether and, leaping out of the window, chased the screaming children all the way back to the village. She could have easily caught and bitten them, but fearing retribution from their parents, limited herself to scaring them away.

The peace lasted several days, giving her the opportunity to concentrate on more immediate problems. Donner had tried his best and was bringing home as much food as he had ever done, but it just wasn't enough now that she was forced to stay with the pups. She couldn't afford to leave them alone in the cab while the children were such a threat, and they were too small to climb up and out, let alone go on long scavenging trips with her. She realised that despite his best efforts and long hours spent away, she would have to find a way to help.

The bench seat that stretched across the cab sat high above the footwell and occasionally one of the pups would fall down into the space and be unable to climb back up unless she came down to help them. It was while doing precisely this that a solution to the problem came to her. If she were to place all the pups in the footwell, they could be left unattended while she made quick journeys in the vicinity to find the extra food they needed. One by one she lowered them down, then returned to the seat and called for them to join her. A pyramid of bodies rose and fell in succession as they trampled over one another in their eagerness to reach her, but to no avail. Satisfied that they would be unable to leave the cab, she left to forage for food.

Cabbie had been gone for about twenty minutes when the first stone struck the side of the lorry, awakening the pups from their slumber. A second stone entered through the open window and rattled its way around the interior, causing them to whimper nervously and look about for their mother's protection. The bombardment increased as the children realised that there was no bark of deterrence being returned from within. Assuming the dog had gone, the eldest of the children came forward and climbed on to the running board. He glanced nervously into the cab – it was empty. He waved to the others who ran forward and climbed on to its flat-back rear.

Down in the footwell the pups remained silent. They knew that when stones were thrown, their mother would bark angrily, but this was new and they didn't know how to react when the round faced creatures came so close. Instead they remained quiet, hoping that their presence would not be noticed.

One of the children leaned in through the open window and was about to pull himself through when he spotted the collection of wide, black eyes looking up at him from below. He shouted at them and the puppies barked back with shrill, excited tones, jumping up and down as if to reach him. The boy soon realised that they couldn't get up on to the seat and teased them, mimicking their yapping, and pulling faces. Soon, the others joined him, until from all sides the jeering faces of the excited children appeared. Together they taunted the pups and took turns prodding them with a long stick so that they were forced to retreat from one corner of the cab floor to the other, tumbling over one another as they did so. But none of the children was brave enough to enter the cab and, becoming angry that they'd have to content themselves with playing on the back, they resorted to throwing handfuls of dirt on to the pups before leaving.

Today, they were going to play mechanics and give the lorry its overhaul. Although the engine had long since been removed, there remained a tangle of connections and pipe ends where it had once been and with a child's imagination there was ample for them to repair. They traced cables to their origin and probed every crevice and open-ended pipe with twigs, while in their minds they were fine-tuning a racing engine with the tools they had seen the mechanics use at the garage. Beneath its belly, one of them slid along on his back, tracing the tangle of pipes and cables that ran along it like the vines that cling to a jungle tree. Using the end of his catapult, he levered at one of the pipes until one end came free then, forcing it backwards, fed half of it back into the metal tank it had come from.

What had started out as a wreck was now further demolished by their 'repairs', leaving the tired and grease-stained children sat upon its back discussing what work each had done. As they spoke, one of them pulled a cigarette from his breast pocket and told how he had seen a tourist throw it away unlit as he rushed for a taxi. They passed it from mouth to mouth, taking turns to pretend to smoke in the various ways they had seen adults do, and applauding each one's efforts. Now was the opportunity for the youngest of them to show his worth to the gang as he produced a twist of silver foil and unwrapped it to reveal two red tipped matches. With not a word spoken, the same thought passed through all their minds.

The eldest child took a match and drew it across the metal floor, but it was damp and only fizzled, before spitting one small flame, then dying. For the second match, he crouched low over it with the cigarette held between his teeth and his other hand cupped, tracing the line of the strike. As soon as it flared, he inhaled, drawing the flame into its tip until a cloud of smoke arose to the cheers of his audience. Sitting up, he spluttered a little then puffed again, as he threw the unwanted match over his shoulder.

The match fell into the small puddle of petrol that had drained from a broken fuel pipe that now hung beneath the truck. The flame took hold and instantly traced the source that fed it, setting alight the dry grass in its path. A whoosh of flames shot upwards and outwards from the side of the lorry. In the time it took the startled children to scream, the flash of ignition had passed, to be replaced by the grey-brown smoke of burning grass. They leaped to the ground, lifting those who had fallen to their feet, before running screaming to the safety of the village. The eldest stopped at the edge of the clearing and looked back to see tall, yellow flames clawing their way around the platform upon which they had been sitting, then ran off to catch up with the others.

Inside the cab, the pups fell silent as they smelt the unfamiliar air that crept in from every crevice around them. Soon its thickness clawed at their throats making them cough and feel dizzy. One danced upon the spot as the heat penetrated the thin metal floor beneath and tried to climb across the others' backs towards the seat above. The others joined in until a frantic wrestling match followed, with brother and sister struggling against each other for survival. They called for their mother, but she was beyond the sound of their voices.

* * *

Cabbie had wandered in a spiral around her home, extending the search a little further away each time she completed a circuit. Eventually she found her prize: an unopened picnic box close to the driveway of a neighbouring hotel. No doubt one of the tourists had set it down as they boarded the excursion bus and forgotten to pick it up again. She carried it back to the track that she knew Donner frequently used to return home, tucked it beneath the hedge, then laid in wait nearby. She wanted Donner to earn the credit for finding it. It would be good for his pride. After about half an hour she was beginning to get anxious about returning to the pups when she saw Donner coming in the distance.

Despite his weary step, he constantly cast his eyes from side to side, searching for the slightest sign of something to eat. When he was about five yards away from the box he stopped, raised his head and smelt the air, left, right, then left again. The smell was definitely coming from the left. He turned toward it and pushed his head beneath the hedge just yards from where the box lay, then worked his way along until he was rewarded with his prize. Cabbie felt relieved that he had not passed it by and now she looked on as he prised the lid open, inspected the contents and, taking nothing for himself, grasped it in his teeth and continued his journey home with a fresh trot in his step. She allowed him to pass by, then emerged from one side as if by chance and called to him. He turned, ran excitedly toward her and presented his find for her to examine. Inside were two chicken legs, a boiled egg and some biscuits. She feigned excitement at his success and licked his mouth in reward then, allowing him to gather up the box, they returned home.

A half dozen villagers stood at the edge of the clearing enjoying the spectacle of the blazing lorry, while the children clung to their parents' sides – the flames' reflection dancing in their bright, young eyes – trembling in nervous anticipation of being discovered as the culprits. The initial blaze from the grass had died down, leaving a blackened circle of burnt stubble about the flame-hidden wreck while, above, black, sooty clouds spiralled through the palm tops. No one made any attempt to extinguish the fire, they simply stood by with brooms and buckets of water to beat down any flames that might spread into the undergrowth and threaten their village. They all heard the high-pitched squeals that broke through the roar of flames every now and then, but assumed it was tortured metal, buckling in the heat. All, that is, except for the children, who knew the truth and hid their faces each time in shame.

As Donner emerged on the far side of the clearing with Cabbie, his precious find dropped from his gaping mouth in disbelief. They had smelt the fire a long way back, but assumed it was one of the many fires the villagers lit to dispose of their rubbish. This fire was their home! As they ran forward, they called to the pups, to be answered by a single, high pitched scream of terror. Donner circled the burning wreck, looking for an opening through the wall of flames, but there was none, while Cabbie sprinted ahead at full speed and threw herself headlong into the flames and through the cab window. Inside it was as black as night and the foul, hot air immediately burnt the lining of her throat. She dropped her front legs into the footwell and immediately sprang back as the red hot metal burnt her paws. Below, only one feeble voice called to her as the sole survivor sat atop his roasting brothers and sisters. Judging the distance to the voice, she leaned forward and grabbed the pup in her teeth then, rushing to the window, threw the pup clear, only to return for another – but they were already dead.

Outside, Donner ran nervously to and fro, pining as he continued to look for a way into the furnace. The villagers moved closer, amused at his antics and – not knowing the tragedy of the situation – assuming he was simply curious about the fire. Then, as if by magic, a black, singed bundle of life passed through the flames and fell at his feet. It was unrecognisable at first, curled into a tight ball, with its face rolled into its stomach, but when two tiny back legs flopped out, he rushed forward to extinguish the smouldering hair with his tongue. Seconds later a bucket of water was emptied on to the survivor as a villager ran forward to help.

Cabbie's hair was aflame, her lungs scorched and her paws cruelly burnt, yet again and again she dropped forward from the now burning seat to rummage through the dead pups for any sign of life. The bricks propped beneath the lorry's axles had become brittle from the heat and, unable to bear the strain any longer, crumbled, dropping the vehicle with a sudden jolt to one side. The unexpected violence of it threw Cabbie into the oven of the footwell, striking her head against the clutch pedal with a blow that knocked her senseless.

By the time the flames had died down and the semi-derelict fire-truck had arrived from town, a crowd of about fifty had gathered, drawn by the plumes of sooty smoke that now drifted out across the bay. As the hose water turned to steam on contact with the red hot metal, Donner looked on, the truth slowly dawning upon him: his mate would not return from the flames.

Alongside him squatted Ngyu, the owner of the nearby hotel. He had seen this dog before, wandering aimlessly around the hotel grounds, and noticed that it was a breed apart from the typical beach dogs that frequented the area. He'd also noticed the collar around his neck and the silver dog licence disc that hung from it and assumed he had run away from home. As one hand stroked the dog's head the other turned the disc over and read the word 'Donner' followed by a telephone number. He recognised the area code as a farming district a half hour's drive away. He puzzled at the strange word. It certainly wasn't any language that he recognised. He looked down at the burnt pup struggling for life between his father's outstretched legs and his heart went out to them. He turned and called towards the villagers who were busy beating down the grass fires with wet brooms. Moments later one of them came forward with an old sarong into which Ngyu lifted the pup, then encouraged Donner to follow him by calling his name as he carried the only survivor of his family towards the hotel. Donner followed, strangely happy to hear the familiar sound of his name being used once again. After all, where else did he have to go now?

10

On the road

The return journey didn't revisit the landmarks that Crusty had noted on the way to the plantation, for Scratch was deliberately leading her away on a parallel course to the coastline before heading back towards the beach. His reason was selfish and simple: he didn't want to lose his new found companion. He had led a solitary life, shunned by the other dogs to the extent that he had never fathered his own litter, and – with the exception of Lim – despised by the two-legs. Scratch feared that once back at the beach, Crusty's true parents would find her and take her away from him or, even worse, a larger, stronger dog would challenge him for her once she came into season. He needed to cement the bond between them away from such influences. His life had been empty and pointless until he had found her, simply drifting from one day to the next and becoming more and more despondent. Now, he awoke each day with a sense of purpose and fell asleep each night with a sense of accomplishment. He glanced sideways at Crusty as she walked alongside him down the dusty, dirt track and felt a glow of pride.

In her turn, Crusty enjoyed his company and worshipped him as her saviour. She didn't see his ugliness, just the qualities that any young pup sought in a good parent. He was a role model for survival; her instincts and full stomach told her that. Ironic as it was, she had been given a better start in life by Scratch than either of her true parents could have provided.

Having walked all morning, they paused beside a small, freshwater stream to slake their thirst and rest a while before continuing. While Crusty dozed, Scratch considered the direction they should take. The path they were following would lead them eventually to the logging camp he'd visited last year, but it meandered around the high land. The more direct route was a straight line over the hills, but would the pup have the stamina for such an arduous climb? Since he was in no hurry, Scratch decided to stick to the path. His mind now settled, he rested in the shade of a tree while the heat of midday passed.

It took them three days to skirt around the hills. As one path led to another and alternatives appeared, Scratch began to doubt his recall of the route. His memory wasn't what it used to be, so that at times he felt like doubling back and taking the path he had ignored. On the fourth day, with still no sign of the camp, he became convinced that he had lost his way. Unconcerned, Crusty kept up the pace he had set, her short legs having to make twice the effort to match his long strides.

It was mid-morning when Crusty first heard the faint sounds of heavy engines in the distance and raised her ears forward. Scratch noticed her reaction, but, try as he might, he could hear nothing. Her younger ears and the training she had received from the blind dog were giving her the advantage. Encouraging her to take the lead, he followed on as she tracked her way towards the distant roar.

An hour later they emerged on to a wide, earth track that had been freshly scraped from the forest floor and led up into the dense, green tangle of trees ahead. Now, they could smell the acrid smoke that drifted lazily through the canopy of trees. A mixture of diesel and slowly burning green vegetation, it clung to the moisture-laden air that hovered over the jungle like a blanket, no more than thirty feet above their heads. As they approached, the throaty roar of the bulldozers increasingly drowned out everything else until there was nothing but a deafening wall of sound. Scratch wondered if it would be the same workmen who had befriended him last year, while Crusty was becoming increasingly nervous about continuing to take the lead. Seeing the hesitancy in her step, he overtook her, looking expectantly around each bend in the road to see if they had arrived.

Finally, the track opened into an expanse of open land, criss-crossed with ruts and gouges where the caterpillar tracks had torn into the flesh of the red earth. Jagged stumps of broken trees jutted skyward, while others smouldered in a jumbled heap, their earth-laden roots like claws. Nearby, spinning metal blades screamed in torment as they tore through the flesh of fresh victims until one by one they fell to the earth with an impact that shook the ground beneath the pup's feet. Scratch took care to steer Crusty away from danger as they negotiated the deep, muddy puddles of rust brown water that had settled in the bulldozer's tracks, until they reached the makeshift wooden shelter that the migrant workers lived in.

Of course, Scratch knew nothing about the economics of migrant labour, all he knew was that these were people who were used to having dogs around the home and had welcomed him into their temporary homes as one of the family before. As they traversed the forest, so they would move their temporary home with them. It was an open-sided longhouse with raised floors, beneath which they lit a smoky fire at night to keep the mosquitoes at bay. The sweat of their labour and the smoke of the fire gave them a body odour offensive to other humans, but reassuring to a dog. These were creatures like themselves, living at the margin of society and working hard to survive. They ate simply upon dried fish, animals they trapped in the jungle, rice and whatever vegetables they could buy from local villagers. Fresh fruit they plucked from the forest, and the boiled water they drank came from the streams that wound their way down through the hills.

The composition of the logging crew changed with time, but there were sufficient of them remaining from last year to recognise the one they called 'the pink dog'. As Scratch passed amongst them, they called to him and to each other, spreading the news that he had returned to visit and introduce his pup to them. Of course it wasn't his pup, but he enjoyed the assumption and accepted the welcome they gave him.

At the longhouse, one of the workers sat cross-legged beside an open fire, frying peanuts with the small dried fish they would eat for lunch and, seeing the dogs, threw another handful into the pan and topped up the rice pot. Scratch settled beside him, accepting a single pat of recognition on the head, while the man made a fuss of the pup. As he stroked her neck, so she turned her head sideways and revealed her bad eye. He stopped and, cupping her head in his hands, gently prised the eyelids apart. He didn't like what he saw and called aloud towards the others as one by one they shut down their noisy machines to take lunch.

As the crew all settled in a circle around the steaming pot, the pup was passed along to a man with a brightly coloured twist of cloth tied about his head. He was older than the others, but had the likely, dancing eyes of a man half his age. There was a perceptible gap between him and the workers either side, suggesting that although one of them, he was also apart from them. Scratch rose to his feet, suspicious of what he saw, but the pup felt the gentleness of the hands that held her and called back that all was well.

This was the 'Moh' – part village doctor, part magician – who combined his collection of herbs and powdered roots with whatever nature provided in the jungle around and could cure almost any ill. The respect with which he was held was earned out of superstitious fear of his incantations and the success he enjoyed from curing the ailments of his kinsfolk. Now, he ran the leathery fingertips of his calloused hands along the puppy's body, feeling for the tell-tale bumps and tender spots that would aid his diagnosis, until finally he reached the eye. The pup began to whimper as he gently prised the lids apart, breaking the crust that had built up and releasing a straw coloured fluid which seeped out from underneath. A comforting hand moved on to Scratch's shoulder as one of the onlookers noticed his concern at the pup's distress.

At last, the Moh returned the pup to Scratch's side and called for one of the others to bring his chest. Moments later a wooden chest the size of a shoe box was placed before him. From a chain around his neck, he produced a small silver key, fitted it in the lock and opened the brass-hinged lid to reveal a neatly segmented tray containing the tools of his trade. He chose three small bottles containing different coloured powders and a small, twisted root, then ground all four together in a stone bowl. Finally, he dripped in a green liquid from another bottle and mixed it all to a paste.

Setting the mixture aside, he joined the others as they ate their meal, talked briefly then transferred to the matting floor of the hut to smoke cigarettes while the dogs ate the leftovers. It was far too hot at that time of the day to work and besides, the medicine needed to mature to strength before being applied. Presently, the dogs joined the workers, lying at their feet, the pup curled between Scratch's outstretched front legs.

It was shortly after three o'clock when the first of the crew rose to pour himself some cool water from a jug hanging in the shade of the single remaining tree nearby. Scratch heard him and barked instinctively then, realising where he was, lowered his head once more. The Moh patted him, as a reward for doing precisely what he expected of a guard dog, then remembered the medicine he had set aside. He lifted Crusty across his lap and sat her in the hollow formed between his thighs. Then, as one hand held her small head still, the other applied half of the green paste over and around the swollen eye. The pup squirmed beneath him, attempting to wriggle free, but, gentle pressure from the Moh's thighs held her firm. Finally, in a small concession to modern medicine – a lint bandage was wound over the eye and around the head to keep the poultice in place. Satisfied with his efforts, the Moh returned Crusty to the matting and waited. As soon as her paw came up to pull at the bandage, he stabbed at it with the tip of spiky thorn that formed one of the many tools of his trade. The pup yelped, more in surprise than pain, then, hesitating slightly, again lifted her paw. Once more she felt the sharp stab of the thorn. And so it went on intermittently until she slowly accepted the inevitable and left the bandage alone.

Scratch thought about the hot liquid that Lim had rubbed into his body when he was ill and understood the concept. In the same way as he would seek out and chew different grasses when he was feeling unwell, so too the two-legs had their 'grasses' and were sharing their power with them. On the next occasion that Crusty lifted her paw, it was not the Moh, but Scratch who chastised her, nipping at her paw with his front teeth.

The Moh smiled to himself, satisfied in his mind that the father now understood and would take care of his daughter's bandage for her. He arose, drank also from the jug and returned to his work. Moments later, the roar of diesel engines broke the peace of the afternoon as one by one the workers returned to their labours.

Not wanting to appear lazy, Scratch followed after them, keeping a safe distance from their vehicles and the falling trees and making conspicuous forays as they advanced into the jungle, as if to show that he was scouting the area for unwelcome visitors. Not that there would be any of course, as the deafening noise would have scared away animals for miles around, but it would help to justify his purpose in being there when mealtimes came around. Crusty followed his lead, advancing alongside him ever deeper into the virgin forest, until finally, as the light began to fail and the shadows lay long across the forest floor, one by one the engines shut down for the day.

The following day, the workers arose early to resume their labours. The two dogs accompanied one of them as he advanced into the forest ahead of the others with a pot of yellow paint. On selected trees he painted a yellow cross and an arrow to indicate which should be felled and the direction each should fall. As he stood beside one surveying its girth, Scratch noticed a thin, hanging vine that swung a little too awkwardly in the breeze that passed between the trees. His eyes narrowed as he saw it curl towards the man. Barking, he ran forward, staring up into the tree. The worker stared at him, puzzled.

The snake curled its body ever closer and poised to strike. Again Scratch barked and this time leapt into the air, his snapping jaws falling hopelessly short of the snake above. But it was sufficient to turn the man's gaze from the dog to the tree. As he recognised the danger, he stumbled backwards, drawing his parang from its sheath. In a single, practised swing of its eighteen inch blade, he parted the snake's head from its body, pulled the remainder down from the tree and hung it like a trophy about his neck. Crusty moved in toward the head, sniffing at the gaping jaws. In an instant the man's foot pushed her to one side, for he believed the stories he'd heard of dead snakes biting.

Back at camp for lunch, the story was retold to the others with much gesticulation and animal mimicry. He portrayed the evil eyed snake and heroic dog with all the craft of an actor, saving the main accolade for the demonstration of his own skill at avoiding its venomous bite. The snake was skinned, chopped into chunks and its flesh rubbed with spices in preparation for a special evening meal. It was good to have the dogs about, they decided, for not only did they protect them and the campsite, but they brought good food to the pot as well.

After lunch, the Moh removed the dressing from the pup's eye. As he gently lifted it away, the now hardened paste lifted with it the dried discharge, revealing an opaque eye beneath. It was clear that the damage had already been done and even his powers could not restore sight to the blind. But, to ensure the infection did not return, he applied the remainder of the paste and once again bound it into place.

The two dogs stayed with the loggers for three weeks, moving with them as they worked their way even deeper into the seemingly endless forest. But, as they took the longhouse down for the third time, Scratch finally decided it was time to move on. Crusty's bandage had been removed at the end of the second week and, with no return of the infection, he knew there was no reason to stay any longer.

As the loggers busied themselves loading the components of their longhouse on to one of their trucks, he led the way across the rutted track, past the piles of neatly stacked logs and away from the sounds and smells of man towards the song of insect and bird in the jungle beyond.

They walked into the early evening, stopping only for water, until they reached a point where the soil of the track gave way to the tarmac of a road. A derelict hut provided shelter from the heavy rain overnight, and next morning they rose to find steaming puddles of water blocking their way. They walked out into the morning sunlight, and considered their first priority – food. Scratch sniffed the air but with no clues to follow, turned in the only direction that offered hope: the empty, black road ahead. He yawned and stretched, watching as Crusty copied him. As Scratch lapped at one of the puddles, so too did the puppy. A belly full of water certainly wasn't nourishing, but it filled the void for a short while and satisfied the initial pangs of hunger a little.

By now the black tarmac was heating up, so they walked along the verge, stopping every once in a while to investigate an interesting smell or study a sound that carried in the air. The landscape was devoid of habitation, with thick jungle along one side of the road, and a neatly set out plantation of oil palms in regimented columns along the other. Whenever a break in the wall of jungle appeared, Scratch would raise himself to his full height and look into the distance for a landmark to steer by.

By mid-morning the heat was affecting them both and the water had long since drained from their stomachs. Scratch licked his lips and settled in the shade of a tree to rest for a while. It had been quite a while since he had made such an adventurous journey away and it was dawning upon him that he wasn't as young as he used to be. In the past he would have walked through to midday before resting, but now his joints ached and the pads of his feet were sore. Crusty was tired too, but in contrast to her ageing mentor, was gaining in strength day by day. At times she even took the lead as his pace slowed, until, realising that she had no idea where they were headed, she would have to stop and wait for him to catch up.

Scratch didn't care *where* they were heading, he was simply stalling for time to keep his charge with him until he was sure she wouldn't leave. But her stopping to wait for him was a good sign. It reassured him that she cared. A familiar ache in his stomach reminded Scratch that they needed food. They'd eaten well with the loggers; more than they should have. He knew from years of experience that it was unwise to gorge yourself, for it stretched the stomach and made you feel hollow for the days that followed on a normal, sparse diet. It was far better to eat sufficiently, then bury the food and return to it later. But circumstances had dictated that they move on, so this hadn't been an option. Trying to ignore the rumble from his stomach, he pulled Crusty close, intending to lick her eye clean, forgetting that the infection had now gone.

After ten minutes or so, Crusty's ears pricked up. Scratch followed her gaze along the road and saw the shape of a small truck in the distance.

As the vehicle drew closer, Scratch reached for the skin at the back of Crusty's neck and tried to lift her as he would a young pup. But Crusty had grown up quickly and the previously loose folds of skin now stretched flat across a layer of fat and muscle. Still he persevered and, trusting him, she offered no resistance. So, as the farm truck approached, he stood beside the road, a fat pup dangling clumsily from his mouth, and gave a practised, lost dog look to the driver.

The truck slowed and sounded its frail, tinny horn. A leathery head poked out of the window to study the unusual duo. The old farmer had the face of a man who had spent a lifetime working beneath the sun. A hard lifetime. A lifetime where animals took a poor second place to the welfare of his family. He waved his arm dismissively and spat toward them as he drove on by.

Disappointed, Scratch lowered the pup to the floor and

waited to see if there was another vehicle coming up behind. A sudden screech of rubber snapped his head back in the direction of the truck. His muscles tensed in anticipation of danger as the farmer stepped down from the high cab door and turned to face them. Scratch had learnt from an early age that there was no understanding two-legs; some, like Lim, were as kind as any dog could hope for, while others seemed to take great pleasure in making a difficult life a painful one too. Just as he moved forward to cover the pup from attack, a second two-leg, a female, appeared from around the other side of the truck and joined the farmer. He hesitated for a moment, then ducked as she took her straw hat from her head and slapped him about the face with it. It was clear to Scratch now who the boss was in their den.

Like a dog with its tail between its legs, the farmer approached with outstretched hand as his wife hovered to one side of him, her hat still held menacingly above him. Realising that circumstances had changed, Scratch stepped back, lifted the pup in his jaws once more and threw an even better lost dog look than before. It worked! The woman overtook her husband and came closer, making cooing noises like a bird as she lowered herself to their height. Scratch stepped forward, lowered the oversized pup in front of her, then took two steps back.

Crusty grasped the situation and, keen to show her worth at such deceit, closed the last few steps toward the farmer's wife with a fake limp, just as she'd seen Scratch do. The woman's hand came out to lift her injured paw from the road and, as she whimpered with imagined pain, a warm sense of pride passed through Scratch at his protégé's performance.

Cradling Crusty in her arms as though holding a baby, the farmer's wife rocked the pup gently to and fro, while Scratch contemplated the meal that would soon slide into his empty stomach.

They'd had to endure an hour's journey before they at last reached the farm and the prospect of a meal. Crusty had ridden in the cab, enduring the smothering affection of the farmer's wife, while Scratch had been relegated to the open back of the truck. Sitting on top of a pile of sacks he watched her through the back window and saw that all was well.

When they finally arrived, they were led to the back of the house where they waited eagerly as from within came the sounds of pots being scraped empty. Moments later the woman appeared with two shiny, green banana leaves upon which she had heaped the leftovers of a meal. It was mostly rice with occasional threads of meat, but the dogs knew better than to turn up their noses and attacked it with an eagerness intended to display the need for another meal very soon. This time with more meat in it!

Of the two dogs, it was inevitable that Scratch would be the neglected and unwelcome one. Crusty was free to explore wherever she chose while Scratch, with his unhygienic looking, blotchy pink body was restricted to the yard. If she was with the wife, Scratch knew that he needn't worry, but whenever the man was about, Scratch did his best to remain within earshot, in case the pup needed help. He'd learnt over the years that first impressions were usually correct, and someone who spat at a dog for no reason had to be treated with constant caution. So, over the next few days, whenever the wife collected the pup from him, Scratch would hover cautiously by the back door until she was safely returned. On several occasions he crept inside and watched in amazement as Crusty was fussed and cosseted by the woman: brushing her coat through, fanning her from the heat with a newspaper, spoon-feeding her from a tin can.

Crusty knew when she was on to a good thing and put up with the smothering attention so long as the food kept coming. Even in her short life, she could remember the times when she had lain in the den with her brothers and sisters wondering if there was going to be any food brought home for them that day. This was luxury indeed, but luxury at a price.

On the fifth evening, when the farmer and his wife went to bed and she was returned to the backyard with Scratch, Crusty realised how selfish she had been. For there beside him was a banana leaf stacked with dried-up, leftover rice, while inside she had been feasting upon tins of meat. It was time to move on. She looked up at the bright moon that lit the sky about them and, with no further hesitation, made her way through the open back gate, leaving the half-sleeping Scratch looking after her with a puzzled expression. By the time he too had reached the gate, she was already some way along the path that led to the road, moving at a brisk, determined pace.

Starting to think for herself now, she was also growing up before his eyes. Soon she would be ready to make the decision he was dreading. Now the tables had turned, for he followed in her footsteps for the rest of their journey.

And, as they reached the point where the path met the road, he stopped instinctively and looked out to the east, where the moon hung over the distant sea. The time had come to return to the beach.

11

A new beginning

For Donner it was almost like being back with his master, for now there was someone to care for him, and the food that he had so desperately sought for his family was once more delivered on a plate. He'd been wormed and de-ticked by the vet and given a course of multi-vitamins to restore his health so that, in less than a week, his bulk was already showing signs of returning. As for the youngster – the crisp, burnt hair had been brushed away and new hair was beginning to grow through to take its place. Here and there across his back and on the pads of his feet were the remnants of blisters from the fire, but they were rubbed daily with ointment and covered in bandages so soon he was able to move about without too much discomfort.

Ngyu was a conscientious, family oriented, middle-aged

man with the gently-swelling stomach that often comes with prosperity. He had built his hotel from modest beginnings to one of the most sought-after in the resort where guests were welcomed as an extension of the family.

He was a good man but, though he had thought long and hard about calling the telephone number etched upon the dog's disc, as each day passed and Donner became more friendly towards him, he found it an easy task to ignore. At first Donner had been guarded, thinking that Ngyu was trying to steal his pup but, as the hand that fed him made no attempt to separate them, Donner came to realise that this two-leg could be trusted.

As each day passed, Donner felt his memories of freedom fading. So much had happened in such a short space of time that it seemed hard to believe it had really happened at all. But, every night just before falling asleep, he was reminded of the comfort of Cabbie's body alongside his own and the all too brief time they had shared together. But there was living proof of their union in the bundle of inquisitive fun now exhausted and sleeping beside him. Donner was proud to be a father but he knew that his skills in providing for Cabbie and the pups had been sadly lacking. He recalled how ashamed he had felt at his inadequacies, and wondered how long it would have lasted. Perhaps in time Cabbie would have found a better provider than him, or perhaps he would have faced up to his failure and returned to the fence and his master once more. But now the tables had turned and he was back at the top; now he'd show the beach dogs who was boss. And he'd bring up his son the same way.

Together, they would make a formidable duo. It was time, he decided, to start earning his keep. Tomorrow he would find something useful to do for his new master, in return for the home he had given them.

Early next morning, Donner was up and about, exploring first the perimeter of the hotel grounds then weaving his way back and forth until he'd created a map in his mind of the surrounding area. His nature and training was that of a guard dog, so it was inevitable that he would end up guarding the estate not only from human intruders by night, but from scavenging beach dogs by day. Donner knew that if he wanted to continue to secure the rewards of a full stomach and a safe home for his son, he had to be prepared to do whatever was necessary. He had changed allegiances and become part of the established order. He was a patrol dog.

Ngyu kept a catapult beneath the counter of the beachfront bar to scare off the stray dogs that pestered his clients. There was one dog in particular he enjoyed firing it at: a bald, pink dog. It was so old and slow that it was an easy target. But he hadn't seen the dog for quite a while now and assumed that he had died. In any event, Donner was working on the beach for him now and he hadn't needed to use his catapult since he'd arrived. All he needed to do was whistle and Donner would come running to see off any intruding beach dogs, some of whom he clearly singled out for a particularly fierce seeing-off, obviously remembering them of old.

Donner's pup had been christened Blitzen by one of the German guests and now as the bandages were off his paws, he joined his father patrolling the hotel grounds. The surroundings were so new and different to him that, keen to learn about his new environment, he studied every fresh object, smelt everything and left his urine scent in a hundred different places. Donner was too protective to allow him to become involved in any fights at such a tender age, and had to repeatedly press the fierce little pup to the ground before running off to engage the stray dogs.

Through observation, Blitzen began to learn the techniques his father employed, knowing that the day would soon come when he would be expected to join in. But, despite having the near perfect appearance of a Dobermann, he *was* a cross-breed and now the inherited genes from his mother's mixed lineage began to cause him confusion. At times he found himself pitying the half-starving dogs his father so enjoyed bullying and, when he had eaten so much that he felt uncomfortable, wishing he had shared some of it with the thin pups of his own age who trailed sleepy-eyed behind their parents along the beach. Instinctively he knew that this was a part of his character he should conceal from his father.

His concerns came to a head one afternoon when he saw three pups passing through the car park toward the back of the kitchen. They were no older than him, but significantly smaller. Whether they had lost their parents or were making one of their first solo journeys away from home, he didn't know, but he could see from their carefree manner that they weren't taking the matter very seriously and that their guard was down. Seeing his first chance to chase off an intruder, he ran forward to challenge them. They were slow in reacting, and he soon overtook them, blocking their escape through the main gate. Trapped, they hovered indecisively, unsure of his intentions. But they must have read something in his body language, for suddenly all three rolled over and kicked out playfully with their legs. They hadn't taken his chase seriously and thought it was all part of a game. All at once, Blitzen was back with his brothers and sisters in the old cab, remembering the hours they had spent during their mother's absence, playing and fighting with each other. He hadn't realised until this moment just how much he missed their company and, forgetting the present momentarily, joined in the game. After several minutes of mock fighting, one of the kitchen staff passed by and stood in bewilderment at the spectacle, before calling sternly to Blitzen. The pups immediately ran for the gate, leaving the confused Blitzen wondering if he had done wrong. From now on he would meet his new friends in secret, away from prying eyes.

Blitzen's recovery was soon complete and he was rapidly putting on weight, thanks to the generous leftovers he received from the kitchen. Gone were the rolls of puppy fat, now replaced by sleek muscle which gave definition to his body and made him look like a miniature version of his father. Although not yet trusted to tackle any intruding beach dogs by himself, he was at last given the freedom to roam the hotel and its grounds as he pleased. Both he and his father now wore new licence tags on their collars, engraved with their names and Ngyu's details.

One afternoon, after Donner had finished overseeing the delivery truck at the rear of the restaurant, he made his way back to the pool, expecting to see his son in his usual position – sleeping beneath one of the parasols. But he was nowhere to be seen. A check of the cool, marble floor of the hotel lobby – his second favourite place – was also without result. Taking the long route through the kitchen corridor and out to the beach bar still Donner found no trace of him. Beginning to be concerned, he quickened his pace as he ran out on to the beach and looked in both directions. Nothing! He ran to the boundary with the next hotel and crossed straight over without hesitation as he looked into the distance for any sign of him.

From behind a tree, the hotel's patrol dog emerged. He was large and tough but not stupid. Seeing who it was, he quickly ducked back into place behind the tree and hoped that no-one had noticed. Had it been any other neighbouring patrol dog that had come on to his stretch of beach, he would have challenged them, albeit far less aggressively than he would a beach dog, but he knew that to challenge Donner was asking for trouble.

Donner covered another fifty yards or so before giving up and sprinting back to search in the opposite direction. Again nothing. Where could Blitzen have got to? Puzzled, Donner considered the possibilities. Their master had only ever taken him off the premises once, and that was to go into town in the van. Perhaps he had decided that Blitzen was now big enough to go and had taken him with him instead. That must be it, he decided and, just to make sure, he ran around to the car park to check that the van had gone.

It hadn't.

Some distance away, from behind the wall that separated the hotel from the public footpath to the beach came the excited yaps and squeals of a game in progress. Blitzen was tugging on one end of a stick, while two young playmates pulled on the other, watched listlessly by a third who lacked the energy to join in. The two pups' combined weight just about matched Blitzen's and they needed every ounce of it to stand any chance of winning. This was no ill-tempered dispute however, but a game between playmates.

Together, the two pups pulled Blitzen forward as the fibres of wood crumbled between his tightly clenched teeth. Suddenly his grip was gone and the prize was theirs. As they dragged it further away, Blitzen prepared to relaunch himself upon it when a sharp, loud bark startled him. All four heads turned to see the menacing presence of Donner staring down at them, not five yards away. They froze, including Blitzen, as Donner walked in amongst them with a slow, swaggering step. A dog such as he, who could intimidate fellow patrol dogs with his mere presence, had a mortifying effect on the beach pups. Anticipating the worst, their minds raced to calculate the best strategy for survival. But Donner was only interested in punishing one puppy . . . Blitzen! First he pushed him down to the floor with the weight of his forelegs, then stood on him, pressing his open, clawed feet into his sides. The first bite was a nip at the flesh at the side of Blitzen's face; the second a chew across the end of his ear; and the third a wide-mouthed grab about the back of his neck that allowed Donner to lift his son bodily into the air and shake him violently from side to side. The pups saw their chance and ran for the trees on the other side of the footpath, while Blitzen suffered in silence, too proud to give his father the satisfaction of knowing how much the punishment was hurting him.

Ngyu noticed the dried blood on Blitzen's head and neck that night and assumed that he had been in his first fight with a beach dog.

'I bet he looks worse than you!' he said with pride as he patted the dog across the shoulders, tossing a piece of cake from the display cabinet as a reward. 'You'll learn,' he continued, looking over at Donner. 'You just follow your father's example.'

Donner ignored his son for several days after that, though at the same time made sure that he never left his sight. He couldn't allow him to continue to mix with the beach dogs. He had to devise a plan to turn him against them. Now was as good a time as any to start.

When he heard his father calling for him after so many days of being ignored, Blitzen took it as a sign of forgiveness and rushed to join him by the pool. They sat side by side, the puppy's head reaching as high as his father's shoulders, and gazed out across the beach.

Presently, a dog appeared on the shoreline and made its way hesitantly forward, looking repeatedly about himself for signs of danger. Donner waited until it had reached the mid-point then stepped forward on to the sand and looked back for his son. Blitzen followed and, as his father broke into a fast walk, then a slow run, and finally a full out run towards the now retreating beach dog, so did he. As they approached the boundary with the next hotel, Blitzen slowed, but Donner barked out for the chase to continue. Staying close on his father's heels they were soon upon the stray, with Donner jumping across its back and biting the back of its head. Both dogs tumbled over, sending a shower of sand into the air, until Donner stood triumphant over his cowering victim. Donner could have gone further and bullied his son into biting the already petrified dog, but this was progress enough for his first chase.

Over the next few days, he made a point of ensuring that Blitzen accompanied him in all challenges and chases. As far as the run was concerned, he had no doubts about his son's increasing agility and speed, but once the point of capture had been reached, he noticed how he backed off, preferring to let his father mete out the punishment. Donner knew that, left to guard the beach by himself, his son would be content simply to chase intruders away. Somehow he had to find a way to make him punish them too.

Blitzen so wanted to please his father. He enjoyed being in his company and running down the beach with him was the high point of any day, but something inside him was holding him back when it came to attacking the beach dogs. Something tied him to these harmless unfortunates; his beach dog heritage – and his mother's blood flowing through his veins.

12

The exception to the rule

Catcher vomited into the sand at the water's edge, retching again and again. She had dragged herself to this quiet area of rocks: and sand, away from the main tourist beach, and now gave herself over to a wave of sickness.

Finally, finished, she made her way slowly up the beach towards the treeline, but not without stumbling once or twice and falling clumsily on to one side. Out of the corner of her eye, Catcher saw a movement in one of the cheap huts set up under the trees. A young female two-leg had seen her and was coming over. As the two-leg approached, Catcher struggled to her feet, fearing the worst. She rushed up the final few yards of sand and practically fell into the bushes.

The young woman called into the bushes after the dog,

but Catcher growled dismissively, neither understanding nor trusting her intentions.

Catcher rested for a while, then moved the short distance inland towards her den, with the woman following quietly and cautiously behind, finally watching from behind a tree as Catcher ducked her head beside a derelict garage and drove herself down into a hole beneath it to be welcomed by the excited squeals of her pups, glad for their mother's return.

Down below, Catcher settled exhausted on to the dirt floor, as the pups milled around for the food they hoped she'd brought. They smelt her acidic breath and, mistaking it for food, made a nuisance of themselves until she finally pushed them away. It had been a hard, tiring day, and she simply hadn't the energy to devote any time to them. The three, three-month-old pups were all that remained of her litter now that Snarl and the youngest had gone. It had been difficult enough to manage *with* Bouncer's help, but alone it was twice as hard. Moving home to this end of the beach had made life safer, but food was harder to come by. And being sick didn't help matters. The pups finally sensed she was not well and, despite their hunger, pushed in alongside her and settled down for yet another sleep, their empty stomachs taking turns to rumble aloud.

They had been settled for no more than a few minutes, when a strange, grating sound could be heard at the den entrance. Catcher immediately awoke and shuffled forward on her belly to take a look in the tunnel. Light filtered through from outside and she saw the face of the two-leg peering down into her home. She had been followed. As she considered the relative merits of attacking or remaining silent, the smell of warm food greeted her nostrils and she heard the rustling of paper outside. Moments later, a stick prodded its way into the tunnel, pushing a hamburger before it. Catcher sniffed it cautiously, fearing a trap, and refused to touch it until the face at the end of the tunnel had disappeared. When it did, she pulled the food the last few inches into the den, sampled it herself, then called the pups forward to eat.

It was two days before Catcher saw the woman again, as she passed along the dirt track that led toward the shops. She was tall for a female, with long brown hair which flowed naturally about her shoulders. Tanned and thin from her travels, she showed an independent confidence that Catcher had become used to among the travellers on her beach. As the two of them came face to face they stopped in recognition and both hesitated for a moment. The woman called gently to the dog and, lowering herself to her height, extended an open hand.

Catcher sniffed it first, to see if it contained any food, then licked it, to show that she was grateful for the two-leg's help. She was over the worst of her sickness now, but wouldn't be fully recovered until she had a few good meals inside her.

The two-leg reached into her plastic shopping bag and pulled out a twist of bread to offer. Catcher sniffed it – no meat – yet, realising that she was in no position to be choosy, took it all the same and chewed it lazily.

Now the woman was patting her hand gently against

her thigh and straightening up, motioning for her to follow.

Catcher looked her over. She'd learnt over the years to be wary of the two-legs, but something about the manner of this one reassured her – she had fed her twice now, so perhaps she could be trusted. Still, as she followed, Catcher lingered two or three yards back, just to be sure.

They arrived at one of the huts and, soon after disappearing inside, the woman re-emerged with a bowl of water and a plate of bones and other scraps.

Catcher ate half, reserving the rest for her pups, then lay alongside her – knowing that two-legs appreciated displays of gratitude – but all the time she kept her eyes open and her ears swivelling for signs of treachery. She knew she was safe from patrol dogs here, for they only worked on the expensive plots of beach, but nevertheless, caution was always the best policy. After a few moments of silence, she heard a strange sound and looked up to see the two-leg holding her hands over her mouth and blowing into a piece of wood.

Catcher liked the thin, gentle warble of the music and began to call the notes herself, adjusting her voice to the tone of the instrument and making the two-leg laugh.

Catcher stayed for half an hour, which was twenty seven minutes longer than she'd normally stay with any two-leg who'd fed her then, gathering up the remnants of the food in her mouth, she returned home to feed her pups.

Later that night, as her pups slept soundly beneath the garage, Catcher listened quietly to the blend of notes and voices carrying the short distance from the beach. There was nothing unusual about this, it often happened, but now there was something familiar in the notes she heard playing and she thought of the friendly two-leg she'd met that day.

Rising to her feet, she padded in the direction of the music and from behind a line of palms, began to join in, straining to catch the notes of the tune. The playing stopped as the young woman from earlier in the day recognised the call of the dog she had befriended. Rising from the circle of two-legs sitting on the sand, she rose and walked in the direction of the voice, continuing to play as she did so. Then, lowering to her knees, she stopped and called gently into the trees.

One of the other two-legs tossed her a cookie which she used to coax the dog forward. Moving cautiously out from the shadows, Catcher settled on the outside of their circle, but once the harmonica began to play again, moved closer towards the woman and sang her song once more.

It was mid-morning and the sticky heat of the day was well-established. Catcher led her three pups around the promontory and sat them on the rocks that overlooked the tourist beach in the distance. Together they watched the to-ing and fro-ing of the ant-like shapes. From here she felt safe, for once she was down in the main beach area she would have the patrol dogs to contend with and no Bouncer to help her. She would never be able to watch over all three pups should there be trouble. For the time being, though, this was as close as she wanted them to get. Once they were bigger, able to run faster and more able to fend for themselves, she would take them back. After all, that was where all the best food was to be had and, with the speed that they were growing at, she would soon be unable to feed them all by herself. She was already making the long, exhausting, two-way journey two or three times a day.

Sandy sat close beside her while Tag and Lady lay flat on the rocks nearby. Sandy's breathing was still a problem, particularly when the humidity was high or after he'd crossed the field of deep grass behind the den. His brother, Tag, was fit and healthy, but lacking in confidence. After Crusty had been thrown out, he had become the runt of the litter. Always reluctant to take the lead in anything, he was always the last in line – tagging along behind the others. Lady was altogether different. To look at her, you could be forgiven for thinking that she wasn't a part of the same litter, for her hair was longer, finer and glossier than the others; her eyes larger and brighter, and she walked gracefully with a gentle sway from side to side. Catcher knew that once she came into season, there would be major problems keeping the other dogs away.

As the cooling sea breeze began to increase in strength, so the waves that broke across the rocks increased in size until it was no longer safe to remain. Catcher led them back toward the village, hoping that there might be some lunchtime visitors to the food stalls that congregated at the park. The sight of a mother leading her pups invariably brought offerings of tit-bits from the customers.

As she weaved her way between the stalls and parked

vehicles, so her pups trailed snake-like behind, casting their large, fluid eyes hopefully in all directions. It was a popular spot for the delivery trucks to stop. Just outside the built-up tourist area, it was frequented only by locals and so had down-to-earth prices. They left their cargo-laden vehicles beneath the relative cool of the trees, to share stories with one another at the stalls, while plunging bamboo skewers of meat, prawn and fishball first into bowls of boiling water and then into various dishes of sauce.

There was one truck in particular that Catcher should have taken care to remember, for dozing on a piece of sack in its open back lay Sultan, the patrol dog from the Blue Lagoon, who'd taken a beating for daring to chase her. His master had taken him along for company on the twice monthly journey to the butane gas depot where he exchanged his empty bottles for new.

As Catcher passed one stall, she heard the familiar call that preceded a scrap of food and turned to face the donor. Her pups had heard the call as well and ran around to her front, each jostling for position as the two-leg flicked some fatty meat from a skewer on to the floor before them. As they turned about the scrap, a passer-by inadvertently trod upon Tag's rear paw, causing a shrill cry of alarm.

Instantly, Sultan sprang to his feet and peered over the rim of the truck side, scanning the area with a furrowed brow of curiosity. He was just in time to see Catcher leading her pups further along the line of stalls. His heart jumped a beat, as he realised that his moment of revenge had at last arrived. Remembering the skill with which she had out-manoeuvred him last time, he decided not to strike until he was as close as he could get. With the cunning of a hunter, he leapt silently down from the far side of the truck and, looking beneath the underside of the parked vehicles, tracked parallel to them until they were clear of interfering two-legs and out in the open.

Catcher crossed a small area of open park towards the next cluster of stalls, unaware of the danger that lurked in the bushes. As she reached the mid-point, she looked back to check that Tag was keeping up, allowing Sultan to step out ahead of her and block her path. By the time she'd swung her head to the front once more, he was there, stationary but leaning boldly towards her with teeth exposed, ready to pounce. He growled angrily, confirming that he hadn't forgotten their last encounter and reminding himself of the pain of his master's beating.

Catcher knew she was no match for him and, with the pups as her first priority, had no choice but to let him dictate events. All she could do was to be submissive, accept his attack and hope against hope that he might spare her pups from any harm. After all, his anger was against her, not them. With ears folded back close to her head, and her tail tucked up beneath her rear legs, she covered her teeth with her lips and fell to the floor. Rolling on to her back, she exposed her throat to him and waited.

He advanced, straddled her and barked furiously into her face till her eyes shut tightly and she began to whimper. Then, moving down her body, he smelt her, pushing her tail to one side with his nose. She offered no resistance.

The tension was too much for Sandy and he began to lose his breath despite panting hard. His fat belly ballooned and shrank in turn as he desperately pumped air through his lungs to no avail, for it was as though there was no substance to the air he breathed. Sultan regarded the asthma attack as a feeble attempt to challenge him, and threw a single, chesty growl to silence the impudent pup. But that served only to heighten Sandy's anxiety, making him wheeze and gasp all the more. Sultan seized the pup by the side of the neck and shook him, making the little pup's legs flail helplessly about him like a rag doll.

Catcher could remain submissive no longer. Quite prepared to suffer injury herself, she couldn't allow her already dwindling family to suffer further loss. Scrambling to her feet she threw herself across Sultan's back and bit hard into the back of his neck, her tactic being to avoid the frontal onslaught of his claws and jaws. If she could hold on to him long enough to draw his energy, perhaps it would give the pups time enough to escape.

Sultan dumped the gasping pup on to the ground and spun in frantic circles upon himself, snapping repeatedly over his shoulder as he reached for her, while Catcher rode astride his bucking back, her teeth sinking ever deeper into the flesh of his neck. As she held on, she tried to call through clenched teeth for the pups to run, but in any event, the adrenaline was flowing too rapidly through their young bodies to retreat now. They revelled in the defence of their mother, snapping and chewing at Sultan's rear legs with their pin-like teeth. A backward kick by Sultan sent Lady tumbling head over heels, bringing a roar of appreciation from the truckers nearby, who immediately began to slap money-laden hands together, gambling on the outcome.

Across the other side of the park, a dilapidated bus – hand-painted in pastel shades and bedecked with chrome and coloured lights – pulled in beside the kerb. From amongst the passengers who descended came Roz the musical two-leg Catcher had recently befriended. Hearing the cheering and raised voices nearby she turned to see the small crowd that had gathered beyond the stalls. Hoping that it was some form of local entertainment or festival, she pushed her way into the back of the crowd and pressed forward. As she gradually eased her way through to the front, she recognised with a start the bitch she had befriended the day before, locked in combat with a much larger, fitter dog, while her pups scampered around its feet. Like a bucking bronco, the dog beneath snatched and heaved his muscular body in a series of violent jerks which steadily unseated his rider until finally she was hanging down to one side of him. As he spun, so the still clinging bitch spun with him, desperately trying to avoid his thrashing teeth.

Unable to ignore the bitch's plight, Roz ran forward into the impromptu arena and tried to shout them into submission but, oblivious of her presence, the two animals continued to spin on the spot in a frenzy of growls and snarls. Like an audience at a gladiatorial bout, the crowd hurled their abuse at her intervention, while hands shot forward to pull her away, lest they should lose their wager.

Yielding to their clawing hands, she broke through the circle, ran to the nearest food stall and snatched the bucket of washing-up water that hung from a hook.

Catcher's front leg buckled beneath her as she lost her footing, sending her down to the ground with a thud. The crowd cheered and Sultan, seeing his chance, moved in for the kill. With jaws gaping, he threw himself forward on to her neck just as the tip of the wave of water hit him square in the face. Instantly startled, he pulled back, the soapy water stinging his eyes, and shook his head violently from side to side.

Roz charged forward, the galvanised bucket worn over her extended arm like a metal glove and forced its flat end into Sultan's face. The dog bit back, snapping a tooth against the unyielding rim and falling over backwards from the momentum. By the time he had scrambled back to his feet, Roz was already dragging Catcher and her yapping pups away and continuing to wave the bucket menacingly toward him. Exhausted from the effort of unseating her, his eyes stinging and his bleeding mouth hurting, Sultan assessed the situation and turned away towards the trucks. He didn't run, for he wasn't afraid, but strutted confidently, too proud to accept this upset as a defeat, but rather as the second round in an ongoing battle. A battle he was determined ultimately to win.

Catcher wagged her tail in recognition of her rescuer, then licked the back of Roz's hand in appreciation. It was inconceivable to her that any two-leg would take such a risk to protect her. The two exhausted, trembling pups that had fought alongside her, rallied around for their share of the fuss that Roz gave, while the dispersing crowd threw curses in her direction for being an interfering foreigner and spoiling their sport.

But there was one who didn't share in their triumph, for the now still body of Sandy lay on its side a few yards away. Catcher broke away and ran to him, prodding him with her nose and urging him to his feet, but his limp body simply rolled to and fro. Roz knelt alongside and tried to rouse the pup. He was still warm, but there was no pulse. She raised an eyelid to reveal a rolled eye.

Quietly, she laid the body down and stroked the distressed mother.

Lady and Tag came alongside, the sight of their brother's body reminding them of their father's tragic death.

As the two-leg lifted the young body and carried it back to the beach, Catcher and her pups followed close by her heels, three pairs of eyes watching closely her every move. She borrowed a shovel and buried the pup in a hole alongside the abandoned garage where they lived. Then, as the sad-eyed family sniffed at the freshly turned soil where the pup now lay, she drifted quietly away.

The following morning Catcher and her two pups were lying in the sand outside the female two-leg's hut. As soon as they saw her they got up and came forward to greet her. She sat on the step and made a fuss of them: Catcher

153

happy simply to receive attention, the pups pressing their noses into her hands as if looking for something to eat.

And, when Roz gathered her washbag and towel and crossed to the shower block, her three companions followed close behind, setting outside the door to wait for her.

Five minutes later she returned with a towel twisted about her hair to find them sitting there, just as she had left them. They followed her back to her hut, waited while she changed, then accompanied her to the small, beachfront restaurant where she took breakfast.

A low, whitewashed wall separated the eating area from the beach, forcing the family to sit outside while she ate. But Roz chose the table closest to the wall and, succumbing to the doleful puppy eyes, ended up passing most of her breakfast to them. At one point she left her table to fetch sugar for her coffee and was startled to see the owner approaching the dogs with a broom held above his head and anger in his eyes.

Catcher had seen the broom too and was preparing to run before he came within striking distance when Roz stepped in his path and took a hold of the broom. Of course Catcher couldn't understand the words that passed between them, but she knew that, once again, the two-leg was taking their side. Perhaps it was because she was a female like her, and understood the problems of parenting.

The remainder of that week was a difficult time for Roz, for while she was anticipating her final few days on the island, Catcher and her family set about adopting her as their personal guardian and followed her every move.

And they in turn offered her their protection. At night when she slept, Catcher would bring the pups to her porch and spend the night there instead of the den. If anything moved in the night, Catcher would bark into the darkness and make a conspicuous effort to be seen – or at least heard – doing her duty. When Roz awoke in the morning, they were waiting outside, ready to greet her afresh as though it were the first time all over again.

The other travellers began to notice the growing attachment between them and asked her about her companions. Gradually they too got into the habit of saving a few leftovers for the family.

When Roz left the site, the dogs followed as far as they could, sometimes watching her leave on the bus and wondering whether she would come back. But whatever else happened during Roz's day, it always ended with her sitting on the porch with Catcher and her pups. No-one other than she was allowed to touch them; Catcher was very particular about that.

Catcher was just a dog; but a dog who'd lost her mate and who saw in this friendly two-leg the only real hope she had for the continued survival of her family. She had saved them from Sultan, and Catcher needed to enlist her continued support in case he returned.

Roz had worked that much out for herself. But any day now she would be departing and she'd have to face up to leaving them behind without her protection. Had this been the end of her journey, perhaps it would have been a different story. Maybe then she could have shipped them home to Australia with her.

The end of the week came and passed, but Roz didn't leave. Instead she worked behind the bar, delaying the day when she would have to make the decision, but each day that passed made it harder and harder to leave them behind.

Two weeks after Roz's arrival, the day finally came. Catcher watched suspiciously as Roz carried her oversize backpack from the hut and leaned it against the wall beside the bar to bid her farewell to the manager who'd given her a job. Catcher's fallen ears and downcast eyes said it all – she knew she was leaving.

Despite the extra fuss she had made of them that morning with an overflowing plate of sausage and eggs, Roz felt guilty. The trio followed her to the bus stand and sat alongside the bench seat while she waited.

She pulled a plastic bag from a pouch in her backpack and Catcher edged forward, expecting food. Instead she saw a loop of leather which Roz passed around her neck.

Fastening the buckle, she turned the silver dog licence tag over in her fingers to read the inscription of her name and home telephone number on the reverse. Then she called the pups forward.

Reluctant at first, they succumbed when they saw their mother wearing her collar without protest. They of course, were innocent as to its function, but Catcher knew of the magic power within the disc that could protect a dog from thunder-sticks.

When the bus finally came, Roz boarded, taking a window seat, then finding she couldn't bear to look. As the bus left, the three dogs remained in line beside the now vacant bench, watching the swirling dust trailing off into the distance. They knew now that it really was goodbye. Catcher couldn't believe it; she'd worked so hard with this one and still she went away.

There really was no hope of ever escaping from this life.

13

Home again

A combination of instinct and the occasional familiar landmark had guided Scratch back toward Chaweng Beach since they left the logging camp three weeks ago. But for Crusty it hadn't been so easy. Her mind map of the area was far too limited to be able to navigate such distances alone but, as the saltiness of the air increased, she began to take the lead and run ahead of him. They had set off at first light, having spent a sleepless, wet night in the rain-sodden fields on the outskirts of town. The prospect of journey's end and somewhere to shelter had given a final surge to their energy. It was now early morning and there were the first signs of people coming and going on cycles, mopeds, cars and buses. The town was like a magnet, drawing in the poor people from the countryside to prepare its food, clean its hotels and entertain the tourist visitors upon whom they all depended.

Crusty was excited to be back, to have the opportunity of visiting her family and to show off her new found independence. But how would they react to her? And above all how would her mother respond to her after what she'd done? Would she have forgiven her by now? Perhaps it would be better to stay away from them altogether. She could divert to another destination and start afresh. It wasn't too late. It was a hard life on the road, but full of variety and unusual opportunities and, with wise old Scratch to teach her, she could become as adept as him at surviving in any circumstances. With such thoughts jumbling around in her mind, she began to slow her pace as they came to the outskirts of town until, finally, she came to a halt alongside the first house.

Scratch looked curiously at her and wondered why she had stopped. She had been so keen to get back – why was she hesitating now? The pause gave him time to reconsider his position too. How strong was the bond between them? She was now fattened and strong, with a mind of her own. She would be seen as an obvious mate by some beach dog much younger and stronger than he. How would he keep her? Would she leave him once she realised that this old dog had little to offer a young bitch just starting out in life?

They stood motionless alongside each other, each wrapped up in their different apprehensions about continuing further, each looking along the curving road that led into town and the beach beyond as though they were expecting to see something there that would help them decide what to do. With neither of them wanting to make the first move, it was the shrill, metallic note of a moped's horn from behind that startled them back into activity.

If it's going to happen, Scratch thought, it might just as well happen here as somewhere else. At least here he knew who was who.

Elsewhere he would be up against unknown, untested competition. Decided, he started off once more and Crusty soon followed.

From the way Scratch settled on to the square of old carpet conveniently placed beside Lim's back door, Crusty knew that they were at journey's end. This was no temporary resting place, but clearly one of Scratch's regular stops. It was still too early to disturb Lim, so Scratch took the opportunity to catch up on the sleep he had missed from making a dawn start that morning. Wanting to reassure him that she would stay with him now that they were back home, she tried to tuck herself into the gap between his front legs, just as she had done when they first set out, but her added weight made it too tight a squeeze to be comfortable, and so instead she curled up alongside him.

An hour or so later, the increasing roar of passing traffic to the front of the shack woke Scratch from his sleep. Rising from the carpet, he stretched his limbs and wobbled for a moment as his old muscles charged with blood then, climbing the back step, he scratched at the door with his claws. There was silence from within. He tried again and called this time, but again nothing. He sniffed several times at the crack beneath the door and recognised Lim's scent. He was there.

Crusty mounted the step beside him and looked on, full of curiosity as to what manner of two-leg would emerge from within. Judging from the variety she had already encountered with him, anything was possible.

Scratch called again, louder this time but, with no response from within, left the back door and circled around to the front of the shack. Standing up on his back legs, he peered in through the dirty window. Its inside surface was covered in a layer of grease and dust that had accumulated over the years of neglect and made it difficult to see clearly. He could make out the bedroom door, standing half-open, but beyond that only shadows. The front door was secure, with no padlock fastened, so he knew Lim hadn't gone out. Where could he be?

So as not to advertise his presence to the mischievous children of the neighbourhood who liked to tease him, he returned once more to the rear and settled again on the carpet with a sigh of despair.

Another hour passed and again he scratched and called at the back door, but to no avail for Lim was not answering. He had so wanted to show off his adopted pup to Lim and having to wait these final few hours longer seemed to diminish the pride that moment would bring. He remembered the last time he had been here – when he was sick – and how Lim had taken care of him. To find such a good-hearted two-leg was a rarity and he doubted that there could ever be another to replace him.

Just as he was about to give up and move on, there came the sound of footsteps on the timber floor within. The steps approached the door and, with a tortured creak from the rain-swollen timber, it swung open. Lim looked down at Scratch and rubbed his eyes to make sure he wasn't seeing double as the two dogs looked back up at him.

Lowering himself, the old man reached out his hand.

Scratch licked it, then moved to one side as the hand passed beyond him toward the pup. Crusty came forward, trusting that any two-leg friend of Scratch's would not harm her. The hand scratched her chest then, cradling her plump underside, lifted her from the step and into his arms.

Lim turned her head to one side and studied the opaque eye, then passing his hand back and forth alongside it, noticed how it remained transfixed in the same position. He did the same with the good eye and smiled as he saw it trace his movements. Finally he raised her end and looked beneath her. 'So, you old dog,' he called down. 'You've got a lady friend at long last. A little young for you, isn't she?'

From the way in which he handled her and the tone of Lim's voice, Scratch understood and gave a single bark of acknowledgement.

Lim smiled and carried the pup inside.

He spent several moments rummaging through drawers and cupboards until he found a tin of tuna fish and emptied the contents on to a sheet of old newspaper that he placed upon the floor.

He'd missed Scratch during his long absence and had feared the worst. Searching the beach for him without success had served only to make him feel even more alone in the world. Now, watching them eat, he felt comforted by their presence. In particular, the young, blind pup made him realise that it was not only Scratch's and his generation that needed a helping hand, but this youngster too would have difficulty once he and Scratch had passed on.

He sat down on the floor alongside Scratch. 'Why don't you stay here with me and we can take care of her together?'

And so they stayed. Lim discovered a new purpose, a reason to keep going; Scratch had the protection of a two-leg and a secure home where other dogs couldn't reach his pup; and Crusty at last had a family once more.

All that remained now was to put to the test how strong the bond had become between the two dogs. Still reluctant to take the risk, Scratch kept Crusty with him at Lim's shack for the next two days. During the day when Lim went out shopping, they stayed behind, hovering about the back yard and doing nothing in particular until he returned.

After her recent experience of travelling and resting, Crusty wondered whether it was Scratch's intention to stay here for a while and then move on, or to remain. If it was the latter, why was he so timid of venturing further than the backyard? After all, she was anxious to have the opportunity of meeting her family again.

In the evenings, when Lim had his customers to serve, Scratch would diplomatically keep out of the way in the back room, so that he didn't upset them with his presence, while Crusty socialised with them. Not that she needed to beg for tit-bits from them, for Lim made sure they had sufficient to eat, but simply to enjoy their company. She had learned from her travelling experiences and the people they had stayed with that the two-legs were friendly, something that was alien to other beach dogs. No-one objected to her presence, indeed several commented that it made the place seem more homely.

In the back room, listening to the voices next door, Scratch had nothing to occupy him but his thoughts. He knew he wouldn't be able to keep this up for much longer. He'd never stayed more than a day or two with Lim in the past and didn't want to outstay his welcome, but still the doubts persisted about what would happen to his relationship with Crusty now that they were back.

On the morning of the third day, as soon as Lim had left for the market, Scratch called Crusty to him as he led the way out of the yard and off towards the beach. She followed, not knowing whether this was the start of another long journey or just a local trip. It wasn't long before she knew.

A group of four dogs were wandering aimlessly about the beach, awaiting the arrival of the first tourists, when Scratch emerged from the trees with Crusty. Two of them instantly recognised his unique features. So he hadn't died after all, just been away. The other two were too young to have seen him before. Yet their reactions were the same as they stared in disbelief and wonder. How could such a repulsive dog have ever fathered a litter? And where were the other pups? Had only one survived?

Crusty noticed their puzzled expressions and moved up from behind so that she was alongside Scratch where she felt more secure.

'Now will be the first test,' thought Scratch to himself. 'Will they react? Will they come over and try to disturb her?'

Tension increased as the other dogs moved in unison up the beach towards them, eyeing Scratch cautiously to see if he made any sudden moves. He didn't, but continued on his way, trying to look confident and unconcerned by their presence. The dogs stopped five yards short and looked at the puppy again. Now they could clearly see the weight that she carried, and wondered how a pup could have fed so well. There was only one explanation: she must be the pup of one of the well-fed patrol dogs, in which case they disturbed her at their peril. But why was the pup of a patrol dog in the company of the pink dog? There were more questions than answers so, deciding caution was the best policy, they let them pass unhindered.

Scratch was relieved that there had been no incident and, now reassured, set off towards the far end of the bay.

Ngyu paused from stacking bottles of beer in the cooler at the beach bar to check that what he thought he had seen was really there. Yes, it was the pink dog. He was just about to whistle for Donner to come when he remembered his catapult. He hadn't had the opportunity to use it for so many months now that he'd almost forgotten it was still there. The other beach dogs were too quick for him to hit, but the slow, old, pink dog was an easy target. Taking one of his preselected stones from the tray, he loaded it up and waited for him to come into range.

It was still quite early in the day, so the beach was relatively quiet with no sign of patrol dogs. Scratch led Crusty right along the shoreline, so that their paw-prints were erased by the final wash of the waves. He was being cautious, wanting to avoid any challenges from patrol dogs that might threaten her well-being. After all, he reasoned, he'd taken her away from here when she was a small pup, so she'd never had the opportunity to learn of the dangers of a life on the beach that other pups her age would know only too well.

Ngyu waited; they were still too far away. Concentrating on the pink dog, he had assumed that the smaller dog was just another stray, but as they came steadily closer he saw it wasn't a small dog at all, but a fat pup. Most unusual.

He remembered back to the beginning of the year when he had rescued Blitzen and his father and fattened them up. Someone had been doing the same for this young pup. Perhaps it was someone's pet that had gone astray? Whatever the explanation, he wasn't going to let it interfere with his sport and drew back on the rubber.

The stone fell short, with a dull thud that sent a small shower of sand into the air ten yards away from Scratch.

He looked up and, remembering this particular hotel, knew that it had come from the beach bar. But today he wasn't feigning an injury for food for his stomach was already comfortably full, but it served to remind him that now he was back he would have to teach Crusty a whole new range of survival tactics that were peculiar to this place.

Ngyu fired a second and a third stone as they passed on to the next hotel's beach front, missing each time. He couldn't understand it, he normally always hit him! Concluding that the pink dog's long absence must have led to him losing his touch, he tossed the catapult carelessly back on to the shelf and continued stacking the bottles of beer, muttering to himself that next time he would call his dogs to see them off.

So the first day back on the beach passed without event and Scratch's fears proved unfounded. All the dogs they had encountered seemed to have the same bewildered reaction to them and none had tried to interfere. Yet, Scratch still harboured lingering doubts about the weeks and months that lay ahead. So much so, that at the end of each day that followed, instead of taking Crusty to his usual sleeping spots, he always returned her to the relative safety of Lim's backyard.

Crusty had her doubts too for, in the three days she had spent on the beach, she had found no trace of her family and, seeing the danger and hardship that most beach dogs suffered, began to wonder whether any of them survived.

14

Return to Chaweng

Two months had passed since Roz had departed and Catcher felt the time was now right to return to Chaweng Beach. The circle of friends she'd been introduced to around the campfire had slowly diminished with time and with them the supply of scraps they kept to one side for her. It was a difficult task cultivating reliable two-legs and none had been so generous or caring toward her as Roz had been. Catcher knew the value of the silver tags she had placed around their necks as they parted and knew that when she returned to Chaweng, she and her pups would carry the magic that would protect them from the thunder-sticks. But there were other dangers that the disc *couldn't* protect them from, and Sultan was at the top of that list. He'd already killed one of her pups and was likely to kill the remaining two, given the opportunity. So, despite the scarcity of food at this end of the beach, she had held back from returning until she felt the pups had grown sufficiently to make the journey to and fro several times a day and, more importantly, to stand a reasonable chance of escaping should Sultan find them. Now, she decided, they were ready and today was as good a time as any.

The pups awoke that morning assuming they would follow the normal early morning routine of checking the contents of the rubbish bins from the night before, then staring hopefully at the beachside breakfast tables for some traveller to take pity upon them. And so they did, but once they had taken their meagre meal, rather than go to the promontory as usual, Catcher turned along the beach, staring intently ahead as though looking for something in the distance. Instinct told Tag and Lady that she was concerned about something – some danger ahead – and the further they travelled away from their sheltered cove, the more they felt the tension grow. As always, Tag brought up the rear, nervously glancing back over his shoulder to see how far they were travelling from the familiar scenery of home. Each curve of beach that they rounded produced a new vista of ever larger buildings and increasing numbers of two-legs. He noticed how they differed from those back at the ABC huts. They were older, with large stomachs hanging over misshapen, bandy legs that seemed too weak to hold them upright. Their appearance suggested that they had plenty of food to eat, and so, perhaps, some to spare for them as well. He now understood where his mother was leading them and why.

Catcher didn't slow her pace until some forty minutes later, as they neared a line of three flagpoles. She turned and led them up from the beach, between two hotels, past an open drain and through a maze of twisting alleys, until they reached the road that ran parallel to the beach. The stench of rotting garbage smouldering slowly on a damp fire drifted up through the alley behind them, only to be replaced by the fumes of a petrol pump gurgling its contents into a waiting car. These were the sights, sounds and smells that the pups automatically stored away in their memories; for they would need to navigate by day and night and such clues would guide them in the absence of light.

They paused alongside the road, partly to rest a little and partly to allow the pups time to accommodate their eyes and minds from the slow moving waves and calm of the beach to the speed and bustle of the passing vehicles. Catcher had learnt from hard experience the dangers of the road and momentarily allowed her mind to flash back to the day she had lost her mate. The event itself seemed a lifetime away now, yet at the same time she could see it in her mind as fresh as though it were yesterday. The vacant look in her eyes as, for a moment, she remained transfixed, staring into the middle of the road, puzzled her pups, Lady and Tag.

The roar of a passing truck suddenly snapped her out of her melancholy and back to the here and now of survival. She straightened herself, breathed heavily into the fume-laden air and led them through a gap in the traffic to the far side of the road.

This was the Blue Lagoon Hotel. The home of Sultan and the last place she wanted to visit. But to reach the far end of the beach she had to pass either to the front or to the rear of it. The beach side was where the patrol dog would probably spend most of his day, so she chose the road side, using the parked cars and pedestrians on the far pavement to cover her progress. Once safely past the danger zone, she crossed back, ducked into an alleyway and returned to the beach. Crossing the busy road with her pups was a calculated risk, but one she had to take. It was good experience for them, for one day soon they would have to take such risks alone.

From the point where they entered the beach once more there ran a line of about six different hotels, ranging in style and price from moderate bungalows to well-appointed resorts. Littered about the beach were an array of two-legs, too preoccupied with themselves to care about a mother and her children needing help. As they scouted their way along the water's edge, Catcher looked amongst them for any sign of sympathy, but saw none. So instead she turned toward the sea, allowing the blur where sea and sky merged to be a canvas for her thoughts. Coming back to this end of the beach brought with it memories of the past, of Bouncer and the brief, happy time they'd shared together.

Alongside her, the two pups also stared, wondering what it was that their mother could see and they could not.

But there was another pair of eyes now scanning the

beach as well. A pair of jet black eyes that focused upon Catcher and her pups as they dared to enter his territory.

Donner's ears rose either side of his head as he raised himself from a sitting to a standing position and barked a single order across to his son, Blitzen, who lay beneath one of the parasols.

Blitzen was too close to be able to pretend that he hadn't heard it and swung his head to catch his father's gaze toward the shoreline. In the six months since Ngyu had taken him in, there had been an almost constant clash of personality between himself and his father. Physically they were similar, in fact increasingly so now that his puppy fat had given way to the bulk of muscle, but temperamentally, it was as though they were unrelated.

They're doing no harm, Blitzen thought to himself. Why can't he just let them be?

Again Donner barked the order, forcing Blitzen to reluctantly step forward and begin to wind his way through the clumps of tourists towards the trespassers.

Ahead of him, Catcher continued to stare out to sea, unaware of his approach. When he was about twenty yards away, Tag glanced back toward him and called in alarm to his mother. As she turned, she felt her heart jump in her chest, for here was a dog with a dominant presence. His piercing black eyes, short, tight hair and muscular body was like no other dog she had ever see before at Chaweng.

In that moment of startled delay, Blitzen had time to see the despair in her eyes turn to fear – fear of him. Within him there arose the desire to help her and the skinny pups that flanked her. For those brief seconds, the two dogs looked back at each other, each weighing up the situation. Catcher's immediate fear passed as she realised that this was no Sultan; while Blitzen saw in her an image of his own mother. He looked down at the two pups as they jostled for position beside her and remembered the beach dog friends he used to play with behind the wall, until his father had caught them together and punished him.

A resonant double bark boomed out across the beach as Donner lost patience. A glance back was all he needed to be sure of the command as he saw his father starting to edge forward – his body language saying that if he didn't get on with it he would come and do the job himself.

Reluctantly, Blitzen stepped forward and pushed forcefully at Catcher's shoulder with his own, but she simply leaned away and remained on the spot. Becoming more forceful, he body barged into her until she began to side-step away, puzzled by his behaviour, for no patrol dog had ever moved her on so courteously.

This behaviour certainly wasn't what Donner had expected and he remained standing, watching with interest to see how his disobedient son would finish the task he had set him.

Catcher sensed the absence of malice in the patrol dog's manner while the pups looked on, amused, thinking that this was some kind of a game. But when Donner's throaty bark sounded out again, Catcher knew she should take his hint and be on her way.

Once beyond the line of umbrellas that marked the end of the hotel's beach front, she looked back to see the young guard dog continuing to look in her direction, and wondered if the spirit of Bouncer had played a part in protecting them. It was as if Bouncer had momentarily passed into the body of the patrol dog, to save them from harm.

The days that followed were arduous enough for Catcher, let alone her pups. Their absence from Chaweng for so long had meant that other dogs had now taken over her usual haunts – and the scraps of food that otherwise would have been hers. It was like starting out all over again. Toward the end of each day, they made the now familiar return journey to the ABC huts and collapsed exhausted into the den, having walked off what little energy the day's food had given them.

On the third day, while passing down the alley beside OB bungalows, Catcher and her family came face to face once more with Blitzen. His eyes widened in recognition of them and he came bounding forward in greeting. Ever cautious, Catcher was reluctant to trust his apparent friendliness and readied herself for a fight. But she needn't have worried, for he was genuine in his concern for them. He led them to a quiet area at the rear of the premises where the maintenance man had his tool store and spent several moments settling them before hurrying away.

In his absence, Catcher wondered what his true intentions were. Perhaps this was part of some elaborate trap he was preparing and he would return with the much larger patrol dog she had seen him with. Then she remembered the way he had behaved toward her three days ago and the feeling that she'd had of Bouncer's presence. Curiosity and hunger combined and she stayed.

Blitzen returned from the kitchen, having pestered one of the staff until they'd given him a few slices of meat, and lay his present on the floor before them. Tag and Lady pulled aside a slice each without hesitation, but Catcher was a little more cautious and picked up the last slice with her eyes constantly on the Dobermann-cross. Once the food had been eaten, Lady's curiosity got the better of her and she came forward to inspect the stranger. Tag followed, of course, and before long the three of them were rolling about on the grass like old friends. Catcher didn't mind him playing with her pups, but children grow up quickly and she was only too aware of how much extra attention he gave to Lady, the last remaining bitch of her litter. Although thin, she was finely proportioned and intelligent, and would soon come into her first season. But then, she could hardly hope for a better prospective mate for her pup . . .

Sultan was restless. It had been more than four weeks since his master last took him for a ride in the truck and he was bored with the same old familiar scenery around the hotel. He sat alongside the beach bar accepting the snacks that passing tourists tossed him and sighed. He needed a change. Leaving the hotel grounds, he set off along the alleyways that led past the swept-up piles of smouldering rubbish, in search of a stray cat to harass or a rat to chase. But there were none. Like all dogs, he navigated as much by smell as by sight and knew that the petrol pump was fifty yards ahead of him well before he rounded the corner.

Of all the times when she could have passed by, Catcher chose that precise moment to enter the same alley with her pups. They'd had a good day, having managed to steal a roast chicken from an unattended spit that had been laid to one side while the charcoals were replenished, and were looking forward to sleeping off the meal once home. The invisible petrol fumes were the barrier that separated them from each other's scent until, with no more than twenty yards between them, they saw each other. Sultan looked quickly beyond and about them, to see if the female two-leg who'd protected them before was anywhere to be seen. But they were alone.

Catcher had known that this moment would come. It was inevitable that they would meet again and she had prepared herself for the occasion. The pups were stronger and faster than before and, although not faster than Sultan, they were certainly more agile for manoeuvring the twists and turns of the congested alleyways. Obedient to her call, the pups ran off to one side, while Catcher stepped slowly backwards, retreating toward the road and encouraging Sultan forward. Her plan was to lure him into a chase amongst the traffic and hope that his rage would blind him to the dangers.

As he advanced upon her, he stopped momentarily at the point where the pups had departed and looked after them. Catcher called repeatedly, goading him in a 'catch me if you can' style and hoping it would distract him from thoughts of chasing them. He hesitated, weighing up the greater pleasure of savaging her or her pups. Realising his hesitancy, she called again and defiantly paced toward him as though ready to take the offensive. It worked! He ran towards her, kicking up dirt from his heels as he accelerated and barking his battle cry of revenge. She turned on the spot and scampered past the petrol pump, looking between the wheels of a parked lorry for the approaching traffic on the road ahead. To the left were a group of three or four mopeds, while to the right was a heavily laden bus followed by a delivery truck. The timing was good but not perfect. Her brain had already calculated the closing speed and it would be a close thing. Passing the back of the stationary lorry, she swung hard over towards the bus and heard the scrape of Sultan's claws on the tarmac as he skidded around the turn immediately behind her. When the bus was twice its length away, she threw herself across its path, praying that Sultan would follow. A horn bellowed, her heart pounded against her chest wall and her legs stretched as never before, to steal every last inch from her stride.

The driver didn't even bother to brake; he simply sounded his horn and trod down on the accelerator as though it was some kind of sport. As the bus lurched forward, he glanced down to see the first of the two dogs disappear from view beneath the right side of his windscreen and smiled as he waited for the bump.

Ending her final bound on to the far kerb, Catcher slid to a halt and turned to face the road. The bus had passed without stopping, followed by the truck and close on its heels another, but there was no trace of Sultan. As a small procession of varied vehicles passed in either direction, a flickering image appeared of Sultan sitting on his haunches on the kerbside opposite, staring back across the road at her as though he had all the time in the world. Even when the flow of traffic eased, allowing him to cross in safety, he remained there, staring menacingly at her. He was too cunning a dog to fall for such a simple trick. But he'd make her pay. Turning away from her, he returned to the alley and set off in pursuit of the pups.

Out of nowhere a sudden stream of traffic appeared, preventing Catcher from running back across the road for several precious moments. By the time a gap had opened up and she was across, Sultan was lost from sight. Running down the alley, she was aware that he might be turning the tables and luring her into a trap of his own. But if she was wrong, staying put meant ignoring the plight of her pups. She pressed on, her leg muscles trembling in anticipation of the fight that might be waiting around the very next corner. Logically, she thought, the pups would take their usual route back to the beach then head back towards the beach huts and the relative safety of the den. But had they the stamina to outrun Sultan over such distance?

Lady had already considered precisely that point. Even with a headstart they could never hope to outrun Sultan on the flat, neither could they hide in the alleyways, for he was sure to sniff them out. No, the only thing to do was to run where he would least expect them to – to his stretch of beach at the Blue Lagoon Hotel. As they reached the flagpoles, Lady turned hard left, almost falling sideways in the soft sand, while Tag – ever the follower – leaned hard into the turn and came up alongside her. Together they ran, the soft sand sucking the power from their legs until their hearts felt ready to burst. In their minds' eye, the memory of their last encounter with Sultan and of their dead brother, Sandy, drove them on, never daring to look back for fear of what they might see. Finally they passed the line of umbrellas and sunloungers that radiated out from the Blue Lagoon and fell headlong into the bushes that screened the swimming pool. As their lungs sucked in air, the sides of the bushes seemed to breathe in and out in unison, such was their exhaustion. Moments later, two pairs of dark brown eyes peered out from within, hoping against hope that their plan had succeeded.

Sultan doubled back along the alley, having lost the scent he'd followed in a spillage of diesel fuel across the path. There was now a choice of three alleys: two that led directly to the beach and one that ran parallel to it for several hundred yards in the direction of the ABC huts. They wouldn't want to go out on to the open beach so soon, he thought to himself. Far better to take advantage of all the courtyards and turn-offs along the third route. Yes, that's what they'd do, he decided, and set off after them.

Anxious minute stretched into anxious minute as the two pups shivered within the bush, wondering how long to wait and where to go next, and all the time expecting Sultan to come bursting in upon them. All around them the voices and activities of the tourists smothered what little chance they had of hearing their mother's call when it was safe to come out of hiding. And so they waited.

Catcher reached the same junction of alleys moments after Sultan, just in time to see his rear end some hundred yards away and heading toward the distant huts. Her pups would take the usual route, she decided, and ran on toward the beach. When she reached the three flagpoles she paused to gaze along the beach for them, but they were nowhere to be seen. The low, setting sun shone directly into her eyes, forcing her to lower her head to the ground momentarily, where she saw the fresh, curving skid marks and traces of small paws in the sand that led towards the Blue Lagoon. Of course! she thought. The last place he'd think of looking for them.

The scent had gone completely now and every little turn-off that Sultan passed vexed him as to whether he should side-track or keep on going. Determined not to give up so soon, he pressed on as the rage within him grew at his decision not to lie in wait for the mother. They were going to escape him once again.

Catcher had barked into the hotel grounds a half dozen times before the pups heard her and ran jubilantly out from hiding toward her. As they leapt up in greeting, she fell to her side and allowed them to clamber about her head, feverishly licking around her face. Together they celebrated their success in outwitting Sultan, but for how much longer would their luck hold out?

The reunion complete, Catcher positioned herself behind a deck chair as she surveyed the distant, wave-swept curves of the beach. The sun had almost gone from the sky now and she could just make out several dark shapes in the distance, any one of which might be Sultan, so she remained hidden until she could be sure. Eventually she recognised the tell-tale, meandering sweep of a dog searching for a scent and realised that Sultan was heading back in their direction. A return to their home was impossible under the circumstances. They would have to continue further along the beach and spend the night in the open.

From their position, closer to the ground, Lady and Tag hadn't seen Sultan's approach, but their mother's sudden turn and run left them in no doubt as to what was happening, resulting in a panicked scramble after her.

They had celebrated too soon, for the hunt was still on.

15

Divided loyalties

Donner looked across from his position towards Blitzen, amazed at how large he had grown in the past six months, and once again wondered how he would turn out. He feared that there was too much of his mother in him for him ever to become an effective patrol dog. He seemed to have no determination in the way he chased off beach dogs and simply ran at their heels, when he was easily capable of overtaking and running circles around them. Instead of rushing out of nowhere and giving them a bite they would remember, he would announce his presence with a bark and scare them off, as if doing whatever was necessary without actually getting involved.

It seemed like a lifetime ago now that he and Cabbie had been together. Blitzen was the sole reminder of that period in his life and it was that affectionate memory that stopped him from enforcing his will too severely upon his son. He remembered how he had followed his instincts and answered the call in the night, how he had run to the fence and their noses had first touched, and how she had led him back to her home in the lorry. Then came the memory that he hated, the one he had tried so hard to forget, but somehow never could. It was the image of Cabbie leaping into the flames, never to return.

Donner had reached the stage in life when he was beginning to feel the symptoms of old age and the doubts that they brought about how it would all end. There before him stood his son, young, strong, and – though he was loath to admit it – soon capable of usurping his dominance. Is this how it was all meant to be? Was it all part of some predetermined plan that he should run away from home and become a beach dog, have a family of his own only to lose them, and finally to become the oppressor of his fellow dogs? In Blitzen was the next generation, physically his son, but emotionally and mentally his mother's son. No amount of coercing would ever change that. As with his own life, he knew that destiny would shape Blitzen's future in a way that he could never predict nor control.

Coming from along the far shoreline, a beach dog wandered carelessly close to Blitzen. Donner readied himself to drive it off the sand, then decided to wait and see how Blitzen would react. The dog passed within twenty yards of Blitzen, who simply sat on his haunches and watched it pass. Either the dog was incredibly bold or it knew from past encounters how tolerant this particular patrol dog was. Donner's thigh muscles tightened in anticipation of the chase he would have to make to demonstrate yet again his errant son's responsibilities.

Blitzen looked beyond the dog, as though his eyes had not focused upon it. His body language, clearly read by the intruder, implied that he would take no action so long as the dog simply passed by, but if it dared to venture toward the hotel then he would be compelled to do something.

Donner was angry and, standing up, barked twice in their direction; once for the warning and the second time to command his son forward. Blitzen pretended not to hear and turned his head a quarter turn away. But the beach dog had heard the call and, recognising Donner's aggressive posture, immediately read the situation and froze in its tracks. As Donner ran forward, calling again for his son to join in, the beach dog panicked and, kicking the sand from his heels, sprinted for the treeline at the far end of the bay. There was no way now that Blitzen could continue to ignore the incursion, so he rose and reluctantly ran at half speed toward the point the intruder was making for.

Father and son met at the treeline – too late to catch the beach dog – and stood facing one another as Donner cast a disapproving eye over him. Staring him square in the face, he wanted to bite him, to have the fight that had been brewing between them for too long to hold back any longer, but then he felt the anger melting away as he saw Cabbie's eyes staring back at him. He turned, his head hanging down, unable to bear the memories that the look had brought back. Briefly he remembered Blitzen as the tiny, smouldering body that had been thrown from the flames, then looked back to see the powerful frame that so reminded him of his own youth. He couldn't be angry with Blitzen for simply being like his mother, so, accepting the reality of the situation, he returned to his end of the beach, remembering as he went the hardships he had endured himself as a scavenging beach dog, feeling for once no disappointment that the intruder had escaped.

It hadn't been a tiring day for Donner and Blitzen. The rainy season was approaching and, as the number of tourists declined, so did their workload. The growing winds that warned of the monsoon rains to come lifted the palm fronds almost horizontal then agitated them together to create a constant clatter. Here and there small flurries of sand and dust spiralled up into mini tornadoes that wandered unpredictably about the beach. For the dogs it was a refreshing change from the monotonous, clinging heat and brought with it the promise of a more settled night's sleep.

Donner made yet another circuit of the pool and the rear of the hotel, convinced that he'd picked up the scent of his old rival, Scar, and determined to see him off, while Blitzen sniffed his way about the beach, turning over the litter for any little treats that might have been left behind. It was instinct that made him suddenly look up and along the beach.

Catcher ran at a steady pace, which translated to full

speed for her short-legged pups, for she was reluctant to stop until they'd put as much space as possible between themselves and Sultan. Tag brought up the rear, close to exhaustion but reluctant to show it.

Sultan reached the pool, thoroughly upset with himself for allowing all three to escape. He would go in now, lie alone in his kennel and sulk all evening. But, just as he passed the hedge beside the pool, he caught a faint scent and investigated. Pushing his nose deeper into the bush, he traced it to a small area of trodden-down undergrowth that reeked with the smell of the pups. A surge of excitement ran through him – the chase wasn't over yet! They had been here very recently and, if he was quick, he might still find them. From the bush, he followed the scent down to the beach where, amid an area of flattened sand beside a deck chair, he picked up Catcher's scent as well. From there it led away across the beach, in the opposite direction from the way he'd just come. His spirits restored, he set off at a good speed, determined to make them pay for outsmarting him.

As the gap between Tag and Lady increased, Catcher realised that they'd reached their limit. She ducked into a hollow dug out of the sand so that they could rest out of sight. Tag practically fell over the rim, slid sideways and tumbled into an exhausted heap at the bottom. Lady, already settled in the hollow, cast a sisterly eye of concern over him. Every minute or so, Catcher raised her head to the rim and scanned the beach behind them. It was clear.

Her immediate problem was to distance herself from the Blue Lagoon Hotel; after that she would need to find a safe place to spend the night and somewhere to scavenge for food in the morning. Then her real problems would begin, for they would inevitably have to return along the beach or risk an inland route that crossed the busy highway. She wondered whether she should consider finding a new home, far away from Chaweng. Surely there were other places for a dog to live?

Sultan found faint traces of scent every once in a while that reassured him he was still on their trail. They were staying on the beach and not heading inland, of that he was sure. But where were they heading? Every dozen paces or so he raised his nose from its contour-hugging glide across the surface to check the far distance. What was that? He froze, narrowed his eyes and stared across the empty sand. He could have sworn he saw the top of a dog's head a few hundred yards away, but only for an instant.

Catcher hugged the floor of the hollow, wondering if she'd been seen and what to do next. With only a sudden glimpse of the approaching dog, she couldn't even be sure it was him. Should she stay put and hope it wasn't, take another look to be sure, or make a run for it? She looked at Tag. His little chest was still rising and falling far too quickly for another sustained run. Curious at her mother's behaviour, Lady attempted to look over the rim herself, but was quickly pulled back down and held firmly beneath Catcher's paw.

Sultan could see nothing. Had he imagined it? For the next few minutes he remained motionless, eyes fixed upon the same spot, frightened to blink in case he should miss the moment. Then it happened. A momentary rise and fall of a dot in the sand ahead. He sprang forward and hurtled toward the spot.

Ready or not, the decision had been made for her and Catcher bolted from the hollow, keeping as low as she could while maintaining her speed. Each fully stretched stride she took drew her further and further away from her pups as they valiantly tried to keep up. She knew it was pointless. She couldn't outrun him with the pups, and to even try would make her too exhausted to face him when he did catch up. She knew Sultan had spotted them and this time he wouldn't give up until he was the victor.

Blitzen watched in bewilderment through the falling darkness of early evening as the trio sprinted in the far distance toward him. Who would want to exhaust themselves in such an all out effort? The longer he looked, the more curious he became to know the answer. When they were about fifty metres away, the second dog stopped.

Lady had glanced back several times and each time seen her brother falling further back while Sultan edged ever closer. It was obvious what would happen: Tag would pay the penalty, just as Sandy had the last time they tangled with him. But they were a family and had lost two brothers, a sister and their father already. Enough was enough! She skidded to a halt, reversed direction and accelerated back from where she had come.

Tag was running on pure adrenaline. Every time he looked back, Sultan was getting closer. He knew that his short life was over. It was only a matter of time now. But why was Lady running back to him? Before he had time to consider the thought, she'd flown past him and into the oncoming path of Sultan.

Sultan couldn't believe what he saw. One of the pups had turned and was chasing *him*! His speed faltered for an instant at the confusion, then, as though changing down a gear, he accelerated to meet her head on. As the distance between them shrank, Catcher too came to a halt and began to run to her pups' rescue. But even as she ran, she knew she would get there too late.

Tag was now totally bewildered. Everyone but he was running the wrong way. Had they seen something up ahead that was worse than Sultan behind? Was he heading straight for it? He slid to a halt and, not knowing why, ran with them.

Sultan now had the three of them all heading back toward him. It was too good to be true. Lady was the first to arrive, but she was too small to take seriously, so he ploughed his nose beneath her chest and allowed the speed of their closing to throw her over his head. She spun awkwardly through the air, the sideways impact into the sand knocking the breath from her lungs. Next came Tag, completely exhausted and with no spare energy to fight, offering only token resistance to the jaws that clamped across his narrow back, dragged him along, then with a cruel twist that turned the teeth in his flesh, threw him to one side. Finally, there was Catcher. With no more than three metres separating them, each leapt into the air, twisting in mid-flight to angle their attack, and meeting off-centre in a flurry of flailing limbs and snapping jaws that sent them spiralling down to the ground.

Finally Blitzen recognised the mother and pups he had played with earlier in the week and, overwhelmed with an urge to help them, ran towards the vicious tangle that spun upon itself amid a wall of flying sand.

Donner heard the commotion too and came running from the pool. He looked on with interest to see how his son would fare in seeing the troublemakers off. But as he watched, he realised that one of the dogs was a fellow patrol dog from the Blue Lagoon. What business of his son's was it to help another patrol dog? His duty was here, on his own stretch of beach.

But Donner wasn't the only other dog to hear the fracas. Just as Donner had suspected, Scar had been skulking about the hotel grounds. He now sat behind a line of bushes on the far side of the pool, watching for the outcome of the fight with great interest.

By the time Blitzen arrived at the scene, blood had already been drawn on both sides. Such was the frenzy with which Sultan and Catcher spun around attacking each other that it was impossible for him to make a first move with any degree of accuracy. As he circled them, looking for his moment, brave little Lady came running back with a determination that lacked any trace of tactics. He couldn't allow her to sacrifice herself in such an impetuous effort and instantly threw himself into the fight ahead of her.

Catcher was fighting for her life and completely lacked awareness of anything other than her own survival, so when Blitzen slammed his body into Sultan she turned upon him instead. He suffered her bite into his shoulder, offering no resistance in order to prove his allegiance. His passiveness was noted in an instant as she turned her back on him and twisted to face Sultan. Together they took turns to draw his attention from one side to the other, feigning attacks so that he would never know who would deliver the next bite. Sultan summoned a scream into his bark that bore testimony more to his own confusion than to his aggression. He simply couldn't understand why this patrol dog had taken sides against him.

Anger rose in Donner to a point where he could hold it back no longer. What kind of a son was this that took sides with a beach dog against a fellow patrol dog? Had he gone mad? He would have to go down there and put matters right. He would have to show him, once and for all, how to deal with those scavenging beach dogs.

The stand-off continued as the three dogs exchanged curses and aggressive postures. Sultan saw the approach of Donner and recognised him instantly. How could he have failed to notice the most powerful patrol dog in Chaweng? Then it struck him – the dog that was helping Catcher was his son. This was the end for him! Catcher he could fight; the two of them possibly; but Donner as well? It was beyond belief that he could survive. But Donner's posture wasn't aggressive toward him as he closed the final few yards. Instead of attacking him, Donner took position alongside him and, ignoring his son, directed his growl at

Catcher. Something very strange was happening.

Blitzen knew precisely what was going on: his father was making a point about being a patrol dog; about hating beach dogs; and about proving your loyalty. But was it a bluff? Would his father *really* take sides against him in a fight? *Surely* it was a bluff?

Scar had moved along the treeline until he was no more than thirty yards away from the stand-off and looked on with fascination. He was a cunning fighter and now began to devise a strategy for revenge. He had a score to settle with Donner and he had waited a long time for a moment like this to come along. What better way than to take sides with his son against him? No sooner had the plan been formulated than he was running down to join Blitzen.

Donner had to control the urge to instantly leap upon Scar. He'd been right after all! Scar *had* been skulking around the hotel, and by his actions, clearly hoped that taking sides with Blitzen would punish him in a way that no physical injury could ever do. What was more important to him? To prove a point to his son or risk losing him forever?

The growls between the dogs continued as, playing for time, each weighed up the changing situation for themselves. It was now three against two with each side equally matched on balance. No-one could win! All would come away losers with bad injuries and only Scar would have accomplished something worthwhile.

Donner looked across at the old, female beach dog that his son protected and wondered what the attraction was, not realising that it was her pup, Lady, who had caught his eye. He recalled the happiness he had shared with Cabbie, herself a beach dog, and knew then that he was wrong. Silence befell them as he crossed the divide between them, sat alongside Blitzen and caught Scar with a menacing sidelong stare that clearly said he wasn't welcome.

Lady and Tag were so completely confused by events that they simply looked on in bewilderment, unsure whether to fight, to run or simply to watch and learn from the strange behaviour of these adults.

What plans the confronting dogs had just made in their minds were instantly revised. Scar's strategy had failed. Whatever the outcome of this stand-off, one thing was guaranteed: Donner and Blitzen were not prepared to be divided and would be sure to make the remainder of his life a constant nightmare for daring to try and break them. His informal pact with Blitzen now in tatters, he stepped across to join Sultan. If there was going to be a fight, he could at least halve his injuries by taking an ally.

The two pups had lost it completely. A fight they could understand, but this to-ing and fro-ing was beyond them.

Sultan cast an eye over his new partner. Had this beach dog dared to enter his hotel, they would have fought. It was so much simpler when it was just us and them, he thought to himself. Now he was a patrol dog facing up to two fellow patrol dogs with a beach dog on either side confusing the issue. How did it get to be so complicated? Was he going to let his desire to punish Catcher force him into making a bad situation worse?

Sultan changed sides and sat alongside Donner, leaving

Scar alone and isolated. Opposite him a line of four dogs stared in silence, awaiting his next move. His mind raced, but the thoughts just jumbled together, thrown into disarray by having so badly miscalculated the situation. To fight was suicide; to retreat was shameful and degrading. He chose the latter and slowly edged his battle-scared body away, unable to look the other dogs in the eye as he did so.

But there was a principle at stake here: Donner needed to punish Scar for daring to think that he could possibly come between father and son. He stepped forward from the others and moved with a steady, purposeful stride toward the retreating Scar, while pulling back his lips to reveal his savage teeth, glistening with saliva.

Scar's fear of an all-out attack by the entire group quickly faded as he realised that this would be a one-on-one fight. He remembered the last time he had fought and lost with Donner – during the fight over Cabbie's stolen meat – and how relatively thin Donner had been then. Now he was heavier and stronger, but older and slower too. If he was going to stand any chance of winning this fight, he would need to exploit that weakness. He stopped retreating and placed his hind feet firmly down into the sand then, lowering his front end, lay his ears submissively back on to his head.

Donner intended to mete out punishment to Scar but the extent depended upon his resistance. When he was no more than a pace away, Scar pined submissively, feigning fear of the inevitable. In the moment that it took Donner to consider the offer of unchallenged punishment,

Scar struck. His rear feet dug deeply into the sand as he drove himself upward and on to Donner's neck. His jaws clamped tight across the windpipe, trapping the air in his lungs and starving him of further oxygen. Fortunately, Donner's leather collar took some of the force of the attack and prevented Scar's teeth from penetrating into his artery, but nevertheless he knew that his energy would fade within seconds unless he could breathe soon. As Donner pulled back, he lifted Scar into the air, hoping his own weight would break him free, but his hold was too firm. Donner knew that if he fell on to his back, he would never be able to escape Scar's death grip, so instead he pulled back, dragging Scar sideways beneath him.

Seeing the savagery of the attack, Blitzen ran to his father and, copying the tactic, went straight for Scar's windpipe. As he clamped Scar's airway shut, the others leapt into the fray and together they savaged him from all sides. Even young Tag and Lady joined in, stabbing their young teeth into any area of his flesh they could latch on to.

No longer able to take such injury, Scar released his hold and spun and twisted upon himself to be free of their combined attack. When Donner finally pulled back, so did the others. The blood-stained, limping wreck of a dog that finally ran yelping into the protection of the night had learnt the lesson of his life.

The panting victors licked their blood-stained lips as they regained their breath and checked themselves for injuries. Donner was grateful for their help, but couldn't help feeling that he had failed. He was left with a nagging doubt as to whether he could have won the fight alone.

A strange union of dogs had come together that day. Allegiances and old grudges had been redefined. For Sultan it was an acceptance that the feud with Catcher was at an end, for she now had two powerful allies to protect her. For Donner, the acceptance that he was no longer the invincible dog of his youth and that his son was as much a part of Cabbie as he was of him. And for Blitzen, a respect for his father in allowing him to live his own life in his own way. And, as for Catcher, she was safe. Her feud with Sultan was over, even though he had taken the life of Sandy. Her pup, Lady, now had the most eligible dog in Chaweng as a potential mate, and she now knew at least two stretches of beach where a blind eye would be turned to her scavenging.

It was too late to make the return journey in the dark to the beach huts, and besides Catcher was exhausted from the chase and fight. Looking at her two pups, she decided to spend the night beneath one of the hedges that ran alongside a hotel wall. Once settled she examined each in turn for injuries. Only Tag had any wounds: teeth marks in his back, which she licked clean of any sand or debris. It had been a strange day; an eventful day; and once again she couldn't help feeling that somehow Bouncer had come back to watch over them.

As night closed in upon the now deserted beach, one item lay unnoticed in the disturbed sand where the fight had been: Donner's silver licence disc, torn from his collar by Scar.

* * *

196

Now feeling more confident about being on the beach, Scratch was happy to let Crusty move beyond his immediate vicinity. Initially, the other dogs had treated them with a mixture of suspicion and confusion, but now that had passed and they seemed to accept them as a pair. But whether they regarded them as father and daughter, or thought he had somehow taken a young mate was not so clear. So long as they left him alone, he didn't really mind what they thought. However, what did concern him was the way Crusty would at times run to other dogs and try to mix with them, as if trying to make friends. Invariably she was rejected, for in a society where it was each dog for itself, friendships were not the norm. However, several followed her, forcing Scratch to move back closer to her side and shield her from their attention. What he failed to appreciate was that she had been forced to grow up away from the company of her family and other dogs. She had spent the last four months of her life with the oldest dog on the beach and had missed out on all the normal socialising that a young pup goes through. She was simply trying to understand how to relate to other dogs.

And so it was with some consternation that morning, that he watched her run ahead of him towards a group of three dogs that emerged from behind a hedgerow.

Catcher saw the pup running excitedly toward her and looked about her for the mother that it must surely be running toward, but they were alone. In the final few yards, it slowed, as if suddenly realising that it had made a mistake, and looked quizzically at her.

Crusty wasn't sure, it certainly *looked* like her mother, but this dog seemed much older and more tired-looking than she remembered. She walked the final few paces and cautiously sniffed the air blowing past her, while at the same time studying the two pups beside her. They were smaller than her, but had the same markings – *surely* it must be them? But if it was, where were Snarl and Sandy?

Tag and Lady were the first to realise who the stranger was and ran to greet her, while Catcher, still confused, assumed it must be some friend of theirs that she hadn't seen before. But when the pup pushed up against her, seeking her attention, realisation dawned. It couldn't be, could it? Crusty had died a long time ago. But the puppy's body scent, although masked with other smells, was familiar. And, as it turned its head to one side, she saw the white, glazed eye and knew that this was her child.

Emotions arose within her that she found difficult to resolve. All at once she wanted to smother the pup with affection, while at the same time she wanted to chase her away for being the cause of the downfall of her family. She froze, unable to decide what to do for the best.

Scratch was now very concerned. The display of emotion between the pups was too powerful to ignore and the consequences worried him. He came closer to see what difference his presence would make to Crusty's behaviour.

Catcher recognised the pink dog and would have ordinarily warned him off, for fear that he would infect her family with his ailment, but there was something in the way he approached and looked at Crusty that added to the confusion.

Crusty turned toward him then ran to his side, as if to welcome him to the reunion that she had hoped for for so long. Simply to test that the bond between them was still intact, Scratch licked her behind the ear and she didn't resist.

Catcher was stunned. Of all the dogs to be with, this cursed pup of hers had chosen the oldest, ugliest, most diseased dog she had ever seen. This pup that had been the cause of the decline of her family, had now come back from the dead to shame her. Any other dog would have been acceptable, even a patrol dog, but this . . . this thing . . . She nosed Tag and Lady away from her and drove them past the pink dog. They resisted, desperate to stay with their sister and called to her, but Catcher was adamant, this was no pup of hers.

16

Whose dog now?

A burst of blue smoke shot from the tarmac with a high pitched squeal as the rubber tore from the spinning wheels of the jet's undercarriage. The heavy landing was the final moment of apprehension for the passengers who'd endured an unpleasant ten hour flight from Frankfurt. Amongst them sat Karl Eidmans, feeling strange to be back in the country that he thought he'd never return to. He'd made it a point in life never to repeat experiences. What had passed had passed, and was not to be revisited. And so it was all the more surprising that he should find himself returning to Thailand. He pulled the crumpled letter from his pocket and read it for the hundredth time. Could it really be true, or was it some cruel hoax being played upon him? The coincidence was incredible that a German tourist returning from his Thai holiday should casually discuss the hotel guard dog with a German name with a clerical officer at the agricultural institute. And that the story of Donner should then be repeated in a letter to his secretary. At first, he had decided to let it go, believing that it was just coincidence. But as the days passed and the memory of Donner persisted, Karl knew that he could never forgive himself for abandoning him if it was true.

It was late evening and Ngyu was busy showing one of his new trainee staff how to polish up the cutlery. Pausing for a moment, he looked out across the darkness of the beach to see his two dogs returning from the fight he had heard them having with some strays. He didn't doubt that they were the victors.

Outside on the beach, the dogs had parted company as they approached the hotel. Donner, followed by Blitzen, ducked around the back of the pool to find somewhere quiet to lick his wounds, while Catcher and her pups headed back up the beach, with Sultan leading the way for them. It was difficult for her to accept the situation, after all, he was the dog who had killed Sandy, but she knew that if she wanted to ensure the survival of the remaining two members of her family, she would have to accept the fresh start that had been given her. The stand-off and fight had been a learning curve for them all that day. Who would have believed that a patrol dog would now be escorting a beach dog and her pups along one of the most guarded stretches of beach with impunity? Other beach dogs would, no doubt, look on in utter disbelief at the spectacle. Yet Sultan's motives were not born out of benevolence, but out of fear of what might happen to him were he not to do so. Behaviour based upon fear was fragile, for once that element waned, so too would the behaviour. This was the rule of life amongst the dogs. They were a constantly changing hierarchy of leaders and followers, of bullies and the bullied, and of the fed and the hungry.

Donner sat beneath the shade of a mango tree and attempted to curl his tongue down and beneath his jaw to the puncture wounds in his neck, but with little success. Seeing his difficulty, Blitzen took over the task and, as he licked the salty blood and sand away, Donner took the opportunity to reconsider their relationship. Today's fight had not only caused him injury but, far worse than that, it had affected his self-esteem. He recalled how worthless he had felt when he couldn't provide for Cabbie and the pups and would come home from a day's scavenging with nothing to show for it but the rumbling emptiness of his own stomach. How humiliated he had felt after losing weight and strength until he began to be bullied by the other dogs. And now this – defeat in front of his son. There was no point in trying to deny it, if it had been just Scar and himself, he would have lost the fight. Blitzen might have the strength and speed that he now lacked, but he was still too young and too gullible to be able to handle a cunning, battle-wise dog like Scar. If Blitzen were to take his place, he would need more experience, which wasn't easy given his disposition for leniency.

Meanwhile, in a quiet back road not five hundred metres away, a dog fell sideways against the fence, his feet barely able to carry him another step. The greasy fluid that rose in the back of his throat forewarned him that the next bout of vomiting was about to start. Sliding down the fence, he sank to the ground, dropping his head between his paws and retching painfully as the acid spray shot from his mouth. There was nothing left to bring up, yet still the involuntary spasms rippled up from stomach to throat. He was just an ordinary beach dog with no special features; the result of constant interbreeding that hid any trace of his ancestry. He was painfully thin, his ribs pushing so hard against his shrunken flesh that it seemed as though they would burst through at any moment. His eyes bulged in their bone-rimmed sockets, thread-like capillaries radiating out across the bloodshot surface until there was barely a trace of white remaining. At his rear, a pool of stinking diarrhoea collected as it ran uncontrollably down his hindquarters. With barely enough energy to walk, he hadn't managed to find food for three days and had drunk only filthy water from the puddles he had stumbled past. With his dehydration now at a critical level, it was only a matter of hours before he died.

Two children rode their bicycles side by side along the dirt road and joked about the awful stench that carried in the air, then turning the curve in the path, saw the dog sprawled before them, retching violently and dribbling strands of foaming saliva from its mouth. Curiosity getting the better of them, they stopped, and standing with legs astride their cycles stared at the spectacle of the suffering animal, while he, now semi-conscious, remained oblivious to their presence. Dead dogs were not an uncommon sight for the children but to see one actually dying fuelled their morbid fascination. Then, remembering the stories their parents had told them of mad dogs that would bite you and infect you with their madness, they remounted their cycles and hurried off to tell their family of the find. By the time they had arrived home and told their parents, the dog was dead.

During the night other dogs passed by the corpse, curious to trace the smell, yet frightened to witness too closely the fate that beheld them all in due course. One or two were tempted to pull flesh from it, such was their hunger. While others, smelling the acidity about the dead dog's mouth, wondered about the burning fluid they had recently vomited themselves.

The following morning, the manager of the neighbouring hotel noticed the offensive smell as he passed by the other side of the fence and sent one of his cleaning staff to investigate. The cleaner looked down at the bulging, bloodshot eyes and stains from body fluids at both ends of the emaciated animal. He'd seen this before, about five years ago in a village near to where he grew up. The disease had swept through the village like a plague, killing every dog and then going on to infect neighbouring villages as well. The Health Department shot every stray for miles around and compelled owners to vaccinate the remainder. They had lit fires to burn the corpses, not knowing that the infection remained in the soil, contaminated by the diseased animals' faeces.

He reported his suspicions to the manager, who knowing the effect it could have on the tourist trade, telephoned the Health Department. Personally, he couldn't care less if every single beach dog died – for they were disease-ridden parasites in any event – but he knew only too well what a soft spot the western tourists had for these animals. A resort littered with carcasses was not one they were likely to return to or recommend to their friends.

It was parvo – one of the most virulent animal viruses around. The Health Department had informed the Regional Veterinary Service, in order to gain authority to draw on the contingency budget. The response was surprisingly quick in coming. That very afternoon phase one began as two vehicles were despatched from the municipal depot: the first with a marksman to begin shooting all stray dogs in the Chaweng district, and the second to leaflet all households with details of the vaccination station they would set up for licensed dogs to be brought to. Phase two would extend the perimeter of the kill zone until no more infected dogs were found. While the staff busied themselves implementing the plan, a bulldozer chugged back and forth at the rear of the depot, gouging out a rectangular pit to cremate the corpses that would soon be arriving.

The marksman was a retired police officer who supplemented his meagre pension with whatever odd jobs his friends in the municipal offices could put his way.

During the last monsoon, when the tourists had gone away, he had carried out the cull of stray dogs for them, but that normally only took place about once every two to three years, depending upon the rate they had bred. They would pay him a bounty for every unlicensed dead dog delivered to the depot, so he spent the remainder of the afternoon driving through the area to try and estimate how much he could earn. The hoteliers would be a good source of information as to their current hiding places and numbers, and – since this cull would be during the tourist season – a little liaison to explain the situation would not go amiss and would no doubt earn him a cold beer or two.

As his jeep crept down the backroads and alleys, passing dogs treated it with caution. The pups had no idea who he was, but the older dogs recognised the shape of the vehicle and the low geared whine of its engine as it moved with a hesitant, stop-start deliberation through the backroads. It was rare for any vehicle to drive that slowly, but surely it was too early for the thunder-sticks to come? They only came with the second or third long rains.

Catcher eyed the vehicle suspiciously while her two pups rummaged in the debris beside the upturned rubbish bin. She stared into the open window, expecting to see the tip of a hollow tube poking in her direction, anticipating the call to flee she would have to make and the thunderclap that would follow. But nothing happened. Instead, the driver jutted his unshaven chin in their direction, his tell-tale eyes concealed beneath the peak of his cotton cap, and simply stared beyond and about her, as if looking to see how many of them were about. She studied what little she could see of his face, hoping to spy the signs of danger in his expression, but he turned his head forward as a group of four more dogs came around the curve of the road ahead. She sniffed the air as he passed by and looked on to the flat-back rear of the vehicle for any dead dogs, but it was empty and the only smell she could detect was from the oily fumes that pumped out of its dripping tail pipe. Finally satisfied that she had been mistaken, she returned to the rubbish heap to take whatever was there before the approaching dogs arrived.

Donner paid no attention to the jeep that parked alongside the restaurant and the peak-hatted two-leg who joined his master in conversation at the bar. They drank a beer together without the sound of the cash register, so he guessed it was a friend and not a customer. The stranger pointed here and there and his master led the man to the alleyway that separated his plot of land from his neighbour's. In the time it took to pour the remainder of the glass of golden liquid down his throat he was back in his jeep and heading out of the hotel grounds.

A single shot sounded out across the bay just after dawn. Heads rose from their sleep, both human and canine, and wondered if they'd really heard it or whether it was part of some dream they'd had. Seconds later another –
Craaaaccck!
 In hotel reception areas all around the bay, the night

porters sat by their switchboards waiting for the calls from guests to start. Each had a prepared slip of paper explaining that there was no cause for alarm, it was simply the Health Ministry reducing the number of stray dogs on the beach for the convenience and safety of the guests. It was done at this time of the day to minimise distress to the children of guests and would be over by breakfast time. Of course the real reason was not to be revealed. Once mention was made of an epidemic there would be the inevitable suspicion amongst the tourists that they were at risk of infection.

No longer at the ABC huts where she would have been safe, Catcher knew by the second shot what was happening. Her suspicion of the jeep the day before had been well-founded after all. Not knowing the significance of the thunder, the pups couldn't understand their mother's concern as she nipped their flesh in alarm. She stood alert, staring out through the gap in the hedge toward the beach beyond, but there was nothing to see. Back at ABC she had an underground den, but here, reassured by the protection of Blitzen, she had neglected to take such precautions and slept out in the open, where it was cooler. If the thunder-sticks came any closer, they would have to return to the den.

Craaaack, craaaack! Another two shots sounded off in quick succession, a little louder this time. She twisted her head and swivelled her ears to pinpoint its origin, but without success. Elsewhere, closer to the source, beach dogs ran, fell headlong into the tangle of thick vegetation and scurried beneath whatever cover they could find to hide from the thunder-stick. But the inexperienced pups, particularly those who fended for themselves, were drawn by curiosity toward the sound and the bead of the marksman's rifle.

Donner and Blitzen barked in unison as they stood on their hind legs and pushed against the storeroom door where Ngyu had locked them for the night. Forewarned of the cull, he didn't want to risk losing either of his dogs to the beer-begging ex-policeman who called himself a marksman.

Once the immediate panic was over and every dog within earshot had found a hiding place, the wait began. Ears strained to detect the faintest sound that would warn of the hunter's approach. Then would come the crucial decision: to stay perfectly still and hope that you hadn't been seen, or to run once he came too close and hope you escaped.

The cleaner had just finished washing down the concrete steps at OB Bungalows when Karl Eidmans tip-toed across them and into the reception. The lobby clock showed ten past seven.

'Is the manager about?' he asked expectantly.

'Who is calling?' the receptionist replied tactfully before committing her boss to being present.

'My name is Eidmans, I need to see him urgently about Donner . . . I mean about a dog that works here.' He realised how clumsy he was making it sound when the receptionist wrinkled her nose up in confusion. 'Listen, you have a big dog that lives here, don't you?'

'No sir, we have two dogs here. Have you a complaint about them?'

Karl was momentarily taken aback; perhaps he'd got the wrong hotel. 'No, nothing like that. I think one of the dogs is mine.'

'I'm sorry, sir, I don't understand . . .'

'Well, just tell me where I can find the—'

Before he'd finished the sentence, a voice came from behind him. 'Perhaps I can help you, sir. I am the proprietor of OB Bungalows.'

Karl twisted on the spot to see the smiling face of a short, middle-aged Thai businessman. 'Excellent, yes, you can.' He blurted out the story of his dog's disappearance and the possible sighting of him by a tourist. 'Where is my dog?' he finished. 'Where's Donner?'

Ngyu had dreaded this moment. As time had passed he had thought the likelihood of anyone ever claiming Donner would become remote. Yet here was someone who knew the dog by name and, by the tone of his voice, was intent on claiming him back. 'We have no dog here,' he lied.

Karl pointed at the receptionist. 'She says you have two here.'

The receptionist looked to the floor, afraid that she had said the wrong thing and angered her boss.

Ngyu thought quickly. 'Oh, she means the beach dogs. There are a couple of strays we take pity on, but they don't live here.' He emphasised the word 'live', forced a smile and shrugged his shoulders dismissively. 'How does your dog look, sir?'

'He's a Dobermann, about ten years old, black and about this big,' he said, holding his hand to his waist.

'A dog like that I'd remember,' Ngyu lied. 'These are all small, thin cross breeds.' He turned to the receptionist: 'Have you seen a dog like that?'

'No sir,' she replied, hoping to recover from her earlier mistake.

Ngyu took Karl reassuringly by the arm. 'Why don't you leave your telephone number here and if we see your dog we'll give you a call.' He slid the reception memo pad across the counter to him.

Karl wrote the research station's number on the pad. 'But someone who stayed here about five months ago said he'd seen my dog here, at *this* hotel,' he repeated, pausing to try and make sense of the contradictions. 'I'll be flying back to Germany in a day or two, so if I don't find him now I never will.'

Ngyu read the name and number, tore the page from the pad and pinned it to the noticeboard behind the desk. 'Don't worry, Mr Eidmans, if we see him, you'll be the first to know.'

Still not one hundred percent happy with the explanation, Karl allowed himself to be reassured by the polite cooperation of the Thai hotelier and returned to his van outside. Determined to find Donner, he set off to make enquiries at every hotel in the resort.

Ngyu turned from the lobby and made his way through to the bar and the storeroom at its rear. Just the thought of losing his dogs was enough to make him want to reassure himself that they were still where he'd locked them the night before. But, as he turned into the corridor that ran behind the bar, his heart jumped in his chest. The storeroom door was wide open. He ran inside and flicked on the lights – but the dogs had gone.

The first, early-rising guests coming down to breakfast, laughed aloud at the amusing scene of Ngyu cursing and chasing his barman through the hotel grounds with a broom. But for Ngyu it wasn't funny. His dogs had escaped when the barman unlocked the store at seven o'clock – halfway through the time set aside for the cull.

At just after seven o'clock, the marksman lit a cigarette and paused for a break. A trail of warm, sticky blood ran from the dozen jumbled corpses, over the tailgate of his jeep, and formed a puddle too thick for the sand to swallow. Even at that time of the morning it was warm and the exertion from throwing the bodies into the back of the jeep had caused beads of sweat to break out across his forehead. He mopped his brow with his shirt cuff and surveyed the haul of pups and young dogs. What did size matter? After all, he was paid per animal regardless of age.

Karl drove out on to the main road and wondered where to start his search. The story that had come back to him definitely said OB Bungalows, but with so many bungalow resorts in the area, perhaps there was another with a similar sounding name. To his left came the driveway of the Blue Lagoon Hotel and he swung off the road and up its dirt track. As he pulled to a halt by the main entrance a dog ran around from the side and took up position on one side of the steps that led into the foyer. Karl eyed the dog, it was well-fed and tough-looking, clearly a guard dog, but appeared passive toward him.

Inside, the night porter was just being relieved by the day porter and apologised for the delay. Once the handover was complete, he smiled toward Karl. 'Can I help you, sir?' he enquired.

'Yes, yes, you can. I'm looking for a place around here called OB something or other. I've tried next door, but it's not them. Do you know of any place that sounds similar?'

The porter looked puzzled by the question and called in Thai to one of the cleaners passing by. The cleaner pointed toward OB next door and nodded her head repeatedly.

'There is only one that we know of and that is the one next door,' he replied.

Karl was suspicious now. 'I see you have a guard dog outside, do next door have one as well?'

'Yes, sir. They have two.'

'Two? What do they look like?'

'Big, fine dogs, sir. The best in Chaweng. Better than our dog, Sultan, I'm afraid to say.'

'Ah, yes, Sultan. A good name for a guard dog. Tell me what do they call their dogs?'

The porter called again to the cleaner, but Karl had translated the answer before he had a chance to speak. All he needed to hear was the word 'Donner' to know he had been deceived.

'Can I get through to OB from here?' he asked impatiently.

'Yes, sir.' He pointed behind himself. 'You just go down here to the beach and turn left.'

Karl pulled a handful of notes from his pocket and dropped them on the desk. 'Thank you, you've been most helpful.'

Donner maintained a discreet distance between himself and the jeep as he eyed the tally of beach dogs. He'd seen the thunder-stick in action last year and knew that as a patrol dog he was safe from harm, but nevertheless decided to exercise caution. He watched the driver pause after loading the last of the dogs, then drive off the beach toward the main road. Curiosity getting the better of him, he followed, pausing each time the vehicle stopped beside a potential hiding spot for more dogs. On the third such stop a flash of light and puff of smoke shot into the bushes and a dog broke free from cover, closely followed by two yelping pups. The jeep reversed, slid clumsily into a ditch with its rear wheels and sank a little. Donner watched as the trio ran for the shoreline where the sand was firmer, then turned in the direction of the ABC huts. The jeep's engine whined and the wheels span as it rose and fell, rocking back and forth in the ditch. Finally, with a lurch, it shot forward and accelerated toward the beach in pursuit. What had at first appeared as a spectacle for Donner to witness, suddenly turned into horror as he realised it was Catcher and her pups that were fleeing death. In an instant he'd calculated the speed of the jeep and the distance they could cover before it reached them. They had no chance in the open, they must run for cover. He called to them with his loudest bark, again and again, until Catcher turned to see him and swung up towards the hotel.

The jeep, now only 30 yards away, slid to a halt in the sand and the rifle barrel emerged through its side window. It tracked the fleeing dogs and settled on the closest – Tag. *Craaaack*. The bullet lifted the pup in the air and spun him twice before he fell lifeless into the sand.

Unable to just stand by and witness the slaughter, Donner ran forward, hoping his immunity might protect them also.

The rifle bead settled on Catcher's hindquarters as the sweaty fingertip tightened on the trigger. Then from nowhere came the black bulk of a much larger dog running toward his prey. The rifle bead crossed to the new target and settled on its chest. He paused, judging from its bulk that this was no diseased beach dog but possibly a licensed pet, yet there was no flash of a metal disc about its neck to say so. A moment's indecision, a sweaty fingertip and one too many beers the night before all combined in that instant as the rifle recoiled into his shoulder and Donner's chest exploded.

Then silence.

No longer concerned for herself, Catcher dropped exhausted beside the torn body and tried to lick life into the bloodstained face of her protector while the marksman left his jeep and ran towards them. The exhausted Lady cowered in fear as he approached, fearing the worst as the thunder-stick waved in her direction, while Catcher growled defiantly as she guarded Donner's body.

Using the rifle butt as a lever the marksman turned the body over and sighed with relief to find no tag hanging there, yet ironically, shiny, new tags hung from the necks of the other two dogs. Running back to the dead pup, he kicked it over to see a third disc.

Having found Blitzen beside the pool, Ngyu had come up to the beach, holding him by the collar, when he heard the fresh set of rifle shots. Ahead of him was the jeep and nearby a man standing over what looked like a group of dead dogs. He closed his eyes for a second and prayed that it could not be true, but there was no mistaking the bulk of Donner. His hesitant approach turned to a headlong charge, with Blitzen sprinting ahead of him, as the truth of it dawned upon him. He fell to the sand beside Donner and lifted the limp head from the sand, then, unable to control himself, screamed up into the sky.

'He had no tag . . . no tag!' the marksman babbled out. 'I told you yesterday to keep your dogs in today. It's not my fault.'

As Blitzen nuzzled in close to his father, Ngyu slid a hand between the two dogs, turned the collar in his hands until he saw the broken stitches where the tag had once hung. A rage grew inside of him as he rose to confront the man twice his size. 'You've just cut it off, haven't you? Here, show me your pockets, or did you throw it in the sand? I'll have my staff sift the entire beach if I have to.'

The marksman made the mistake of swearing at him,

which served only to reinforce Ngyu's suspicion. He pulled the rifle from him and threw it to the sand, then launched himself into an uncontrollable frenzy of punches and kicks that sent them both to the ground.

Karl Eidmans came out of the Blue Lagoon and crossed the beach directly into the grounds of OB. He was determined not to be fobbed off a second time. This time he would call the police and have them search the hotel. Ahead of him he saw the hotelier who had lied to him, fighting in the sand with a larger man and ran forward to intervene. When he arrived and recognised the body of his old friend, he fell beside him and hugged the still warm body. 'Donner, Donner,' he cried aloud. 'It's me. I've come to take you home. Don't die on me now that I've found you.' He thought for an instant that Donner's eyes flicked open and his old dog recognised him, but it was probably just wishful thinking, for he could find no pulse.

Donner hadn't heard the shot or felt the pain of the bullet passing through him, but in the final moments that he held on to life he imagined that his son was lying close by him and that his master, Karl, had returned, and his arms were around him once more as he called his name and stroked his throbbing head. But how could that be? Maybe this was what happened when you died. You imagine things how you would like them to be.

The fight stopped as suddenly as it had started as both humans and dogs watched in silence as Karl rocked the cradled body back and forth like a child with a doll, and cried his heart out.

17

The way out

Blitzen was becoming frustrated at being tethered. Ngyu had placed a chain from his collar to a metal ring set in the concrete that gave him an arc of about ten metres to move about in. It was for his own protection, to stop him accidentally wandering out of the hotel grounds and into range of the ongoing cull. But Blitzen felt as though he was being punished and couldn't understand why his master didn't want him to take over the patrolling duties of his father. The frustration, mixed with his sense of loss, resulted in a depression that left him lying immobile on the concrete for hour after hour. His mind just churned over the same thoughts, again and again. He regretted his disobedience to his father and wished now that he could have been the strict patrol dog that his father so wanted him to be, instead of the easy going playmate he enjoyed being. It would have been a small sacrifice to have made, but now it was too late. No longer was he interested in making friends, socialising with the guests or accepting tit-bits from them; his bowl of food lay uneaten beside him and all he seemed to want to do was to sleep.

Blitzen didn't even bother to open his eyes when Ngyu came over and knelt beside him. Only when he felt his hand upon his head did he look wearily up at him. Ngyu remembered the small, flame-charred pup he had carried from the fire in a sarong some six months ago and realised then that this was the final member of that family to survive. He had only caught a glimpse of Blitzen's mother as she leapt into the flames, but had seen enough to know that she was a lean, hungry beach dog. He began to realise that Blitzen had been born between two worlds, with a beach dog mother and a guard dog father. He had known times of hunger and of plenty, and was in every sense of the word, the 'bridge' between the two communities of dogs. Ngyu massaged the back of Blitzen's neck, knowing the relief it brought him and hoping it would do the same for his dog, but Blitzen's only response was to sigh long and slow.

'I know,' he said. 'I miss him too.'

Since losing Tag, Catcher had been lucky in avoiding the patrols. Several times she had tried to make the journey back to the beach huts and the safety of her underground den, but each time had met the thunder-sticks sweeping through the area. At first they only came hunting in the morning and evening, but now it was all the time. Having to remain concealed meant less time for scavenging, and the decreasing population of two-legs on the beach meant even less food. And so she resorted to hunting rats by night. But now when she presented them to the kitchen doors, she was chased away with angry shouting and banging of pots, leaving the rats as their only source of food.

Blitzen heard her call into the hotel grounds and thought he was imagining it. Then the sound came again and he raised himself to look out from beneath the parasol across the pool to the empty beach beyond. He saw nothing but the hundreds of raindrops bursting across the surface of the pool. Again it came and he looked once more, and this time saw something move in the shrubbery alongside the end of the deserted pool. He called back.

Hunger had driven Catcher to desperate measures and she had come begging for food from the only place she could think to go.

Blitzen recognised her as she peered out from her hiding place and sprang from the floor, only to be jerked back by the chain on his collar. He called in response, urging her to come to him.

Catcher was relieved to hear the tone of his reply and, leaving cover, led Lady hesitantly towards him.

He studied their rain-soaked features and, seeing the hunger in their eyes, stepped sideways to reveal the bowl of uneaten food beside him. They needed no invitation and fell eagerly upon its contents. Blitzen looked on, glad that he was able to help, but no sooner had they started to feed than a sudden, brilliant flash of lightning startled them. Immediately suspecting it was the flash of a thunder-stick, Catcher bolted for the shrubbery, with her sole remaining pup directly behind her.

The tourist returned to the hotel and peeled the backing from his polaroid photograph. A fine guard dog this is, he thought to himself, instead of protecting us, it shares its food with rabid scavengers!

Scratch knew only too well what was happening. He'd seen culls about four or five times in his life, but never before the long rains had arrived and never as sustained as this. It seemed as though they were intending to kill every single dog this time. Crusty was his pride and joy and, after working so hard to save her, he wasn't going to let the hunters, or anyone else, take her away from him. With Lim as their source of food, there was no need to go to the beach, so they remained in the relative safety of Lim's backyard.

The decline in tourism had forced the Health Authority to supplement the marksman patrol with two marksmen on foot, who spent as much time talking with the locals as hunting. Local information was vital if they were to track down and eliminate every potential carrier of the virus.

It was mid morning and Lim was away at the market when the foot patrol knocked at neighbouring houses to follow up on reports of a sickly, old dog that had been seen nearby. Crusty was restless, and impatient to go back to the beach and try to meet her family again. Even if her mother wouldn't accept her, there was a chance that she might be able to spend some time with her brother and sister. Like most of the houses in the area, Lim's shack was raised on each corner by concrete blocks which allowed a cooling draught to circulate beneath. He used the space to store old furniture and odds and ends that might someday be useful. While Scratch slept on his piece of carpet, Crusty busied herself investigating every hollow and smell she could find. She was so involved that she didn't hear the footsteps that passed along the back alley or notice the blue-black tip of the rifle barrel that slotted through a gap in the fencing into Lim's backyard.

Lim was making his way home along the shady side of the street, carrying the plastic bag of provisions he had bought in the market. In his pocket he carried the appointment card for the Health Authority visit this afternoon to vaccinate his pets, and the two numbered licence tags that he had just purchased from the booth they had set up outside the post office.

A single rifle shot broke the silence. There was nothing unusual about that, he knew the cull was on, in fact that was what had prompted him to dip into his meagre savings and pay for the licences and vaccine, but this shot was not the normal distant echo coming from the beach, this one was close by. He quickened his step then, turning the corner, saw a man wearing a khaki uniform crouching low at the front of his shack and pulling out the old furniture he had stored there. Suddenly realising what was happening, he dropped his bag of groceries to the floor and ran with his clumsy, limping gait towards them. 'Stop, stop,' he yelled.

Crusty didn't understand what was happening but knew from the angry tone of voice and violent manner with which the two-leg pursued her that it meant trouble. Eventually, he displaced her from beneath the old cupboard and she ducked behind a crate. Yet despite her calls for his help, Scratch was nowhere to be seen.

Lim pulled the marksman away by the shoulder and half-dived, half-fell into the space beneath the shack. 'Leave them alone!' he screamed. 'They're my friends, they're licensed.'

'Friends!' the man replied sarcastically. 'That old, disease-ridden bag of bones is your friend? You sad old man.' He reached forward to pull him out of the way. 'Come on, get out of the way,' he continued. 'I've got a job to do.'

Lim scrambled away between the boxes and rubbish, calling to his dogs. Finally, he lifted one box and pulled the frightened pup into his arms.

'Bring her out here!' the man demanded. 'It's for the benefit of everyone. Don't be selfish.'

Turning his back to the marksman, as though to shield Crusty from any bullet, Lim continued to call for Scratch, whilst pulling the licence discs from his pocket. He threw them out on to the pavement beside the man. 'There, see for yourself. You can't shoot these dogs. They'll be vaccinated this afternoon.'

The marksman picked up the discs and checked them. 'Issued this morning,' he said. 'Pity you didn't get them earlier. Okay, keep the pup, but I'll be back later to clear up and check your vaccination certificate.'

'Keep the pup,' he had said. And 'clear up'. What did he mean? Lim was suddenly overcome with the meaning of his parting words and the realisation of the single shot he had heard. In a crazed panic he fought his way through an obstacle course of old belongings and pulled himself out to the rear of his shack. He cupped the pup's face in his hand and covered its good eye so that it wouldn't have to see Scratch's body lying, just as he had slept, except for the single shot to the brain which had killed him.

Lim pulled the edge of the carpet over his body and went inside. Sitting on the edge of his bed, he stroked the still shivering pup and cried for his old friend. It was a good death, he thought to himself. He wouldn't have felt a thing. It would have been just like not waking from his sleep.

As dark clouds passed overhead and the sea changed from a dark blue to an oily green, a handful of tourists made their way to Ngyu's beachside bar to shelter from the rain. Ngyu was happy to have the business and made a fuss of attending to his customers as they escaped from the downpour.

Once all were served, he circulated his broad smile amongst them and offered snacks. But one girl refused to be cheered by his attention.

'Hey, why so sad? It's only a little rain, it'll soon pass.'

She introduced herself as Roz, and said, 'It's not the rain, it's my dog. A beach dog I met when I was here a few months back. I came to take her back to Sydney with me, but now it's too late. They must have shot her.'

The parallels with his own loss were only too apparent and Ngyu felt a sense of empathy toward her. 'I know exactly how you are feeling.' He settled on the stall alongside her and in a gentle, slow voice told the story of how he had rescued and adopted Donner, and how he had been shot as well.

The sense of shared loss made it a little easier for Roz to bear and, even though the rain cloud had now passed by and the tourists were returning to the beach, she stayed, as they swapped stories of their experiences. 'Do you have a photo of your Donner?' she asked.

'No, and I really regret it now,' he said with a look of disappointment. 'I always intended to but never thought he would only be around for such a short time. But, hold on a moment . . .' He returned to the far side of the bar and rummaged through the odds and ends of paper he kept there. 'One of my customers took a polaroid of Donner's pup, Blitzen. He looks almost identical, except for his size.' He cursed in Thai as a handful of papers fell to the floor. 'Funnily enough, he took the photo to complain about beach dogs coming into the hotel and not being chased away by Blitzen.' Finally he found the crumpled photograph and handed it to Roz.

The photograph shook as Roz's hands trembled with excitement. 'That's her,' she garbled nervously. 'That's my dog with him! Where was this taken?'

'Beside the pool over there,' Ngyu replied as he pointed over his shoulder. 'Come on, I'll introduce you to Blitzen.'

As they crossed to the pool, Roz recognised the scene from the photo. She knelt beside Blitzen, but he remained motionless. 'What's the matter with him? He looks so worn out.'

Ngyu massaged the dog's neck. 'He's been like this ever since Donner was shot.' Then he remembered something and took the polaroid from Roz's hand. 'Yes, I remember now. This dog was there on the day it happened. One of her pups was shot as well, but then she disappeared again.'

'So she could still be alive?'

Ngyu hesitated a little too long for his reply to seem convincing. 'Yes, I guess it's possible.' But, in his mind, he feared she would already have been shot and cremated.

'Do you mind if I hang around for a while, just in case?'

'Please, feel free. As you can see there's little enough business at the moment – it will be nice to have some company.'

Roz spent the remainder of the day in and around the hotel. She searched every nook and cranny of the outbuildings and surrounding vegetation but found no trace of her dog or its sole surviving pup. With so little time left before she flew out, would there be enough time to find her? She was alive – she was sure of it now. And meeting Ngyu was no chance happening, it was meant to happen. For why else would fate bring her to the photo if she was already dead?

Roz ate in the beach bar that evening, then loaded the scraps that Ngyu gave her into a bag and set off for one final search of the area. She left a trail of food in strategic places and returned periodically to see if they had been taken. One or two were taken, but she had no way of knowing which dog had taken it unless she was there at the time. Finally, close to tears, she settled exhausted into one of the sunloungers facing the night sea and began to accept the inevitable. She would never find her dog, and would return home never knowing whether she had given up too soon and abandoned her to the inevitable consequence of the marksman's bullet. Her six months of travel had been the best of her life: the independence, the adventure of each new day and the challenges she had overcome, and the friends she had made from around the world. But the final chapter was missing, for without saving this dog, she felt that she had failed.

Ngyu crept up silently from behind, tapped Roz on the arm and directed her gaze to the pool.

She stared in disbelief as Catcher and her pup fed from Blitzen's bowl, while he lay passively alongside. Not wanting to scare them away, she tip-toed around the bar and came towards the pool from the beach. When she was no more than twenty yards away, she sat in the sand and called to her dogs.

Catcher recognised the tone of voice that meant a dog was being called, but was too preoccupied with feeding to care. An idea suddenly came to Roz and, reaching into her shoulder bag, she took out her harmonica and began to play the tune that Catcher had first sung along to.

Catcher's head rose from the bowl and she looked toward the sound. It can't be, she thought to herself, moving toward the figure with its back now turned toward her. Then she caught the scent in the wind. It really was her! She'd come back! At last someone had come back for her! She mimicked the notes with her strained voice and Roz turned to face her.

As Roz rose from the sand, Catcher sprang forward and sprinted the final few metres between them. Ngyu looked on, his heart in his mouth as the two of them rolled together in the sand, reunited at last.

Epilogue

It had been a confusing time for Catcher. Having known the freedom of the open beach, she had been reluctant to enter the wooden crate, but trusted Roz not to harm her and went inside. Then came the strange sensation of flying, the chilling cold of the aircraft's air-conditioning, and finally the months spent in yet more confinement at the quarantine station. But it was all worthwhile now as she ran with Roz along the Australian beach that was her new home.

Back in Chaweng, Lady had paired off with Blitzen, and together they had become the model for the way forward. No longer a divided community of beach dogs and patrol dogs, all the dogs of Chaweng were healthy and well-fed, thanks to the hard work of 'The Project', a charitable organisation that had been set up by the hoteliers, led by Ngyu, who were determined never again to see the slump in tourism that the cull had caused. Both Karl and Roz promoted the cause in their own countries and acted as fund-raisers. The programme of sterilisation and vaccination sought to manage the population and health of the beach dogs, while a feeding programme utilised the food scraps ordinarily dumped by the hotels and restaurants.

And Lim had found a new purpose in life as he became the Project's first employee – in charge of collecting, processing and distributing the food scraps from the hotels.

And as for Crusty, she surprised everyone when she produced a litter of the healthiest pups that had been seen for a long time. They were the final parting gift of crafty old Scratch.

FAMILY TREE
(brackets = deceased)

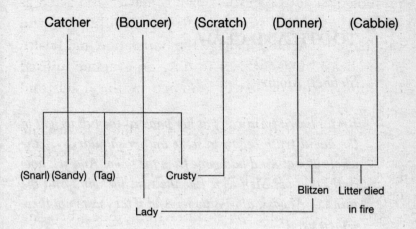

TOOTH AND CLAW

Stephen Moore

Bryna licked frantically at her paws as the full weight of the awful truth began to settle on her shoulders . . . the whole of mankind had gone from the town. And yet, how could that be? Men were like the sun, the wind and the rain . . . Always, always there. And if they were not there – then what?

Abandoned in the depths of winter, the once pampered pets of men, the cats and the dogs, are left to their own fate. To fend for themselves. Can they survive the cruel weather? Most importantly, can they survive each other?

And later, when the empty town reveals its darkest secret, and the hunters become the hunted, it's kill or be killed. To survive, the animals must unite. In the most desperate fight of their lives.

TORN EAR

Geoffrey Malone

The wind carried the scent of blood far into the night, while the vixen still pawed at the broken little bodies on the pile of earth . . .

But Torn Ear survives the gamekeeper's attack. Slowly his mother introduces him to the fox's world – the skills of hunting and how to avoid danger. Then he is on his own.

Until he meets Velvet, and they have their own cubs. But man intervenes again, and his favourite cub is threatened. Torn Ear must rescue her, but will he escape the clutches of the gamekeeper this time?

FINN THE WOLFHOUND

A J Dawson

Finn was bred to be a champion. Suddenly separated from his beloved master, the young dog finds himself alone in a hostile world. Hunted and driven into a savage wilderness, Finn begins the long quest to find his way home.

'*One of the best animal stories in the English Language.*'
Henry Treece